AT THE WILD WEST DUDE SHOW

"Quiet, you rock-candy-eatin' varmint, you," Sam said to Stevie. He grabbed her by the shoulder. Stevie could see Kate and Chuck nearby. They were almost to the part of the show where Chuck and Sam mounted their horses and began their escape. "Okay, now, I'm tellin' you that if you make one false move, you're dead," Sam growled to Stevie. "So if I was you, I'd let out one mighty powerful scream just about now."

Obediently, Stevie opened her mouth and let out her most bloodcurdling shriek. Just then, out of the corner of her eye, she spotted Stewball again. And this time the horse wasn't just watching. He whinnied and reared, snapping the lead holding him to the hitching post. He reared again, and then, apparently realizing he was free, he galloped straight toward her!

THE SADDLE CLUB

HORSE TALE

BONNIE BRYANT

A SKYLARK BOOK
NEW YORK · TORONTO · LONDON · SYDNEY · AUCKLAND

RL 5, 009–012

HORSE TALE

A Bantam Skylark Book / August 1994

*Skylark Books is a registered trademark of Bantam Books,
a division of Bantam Doubleday Dell Publishing Group, Inc.
Registered in U.S. Patent and Trademark Office and elsewhere.*

*"The Saddle Club" is a registered trademark of Bonnie Bryant Hiller.
The Saddle Club design / logo, which consists of a riding crop
and a riding hat, is a trademark of Bantam Books.*

ISBN 0-553-48150-9

Published simultaneously in the United States and Canada

*Bantam Books are published by Bantam Books, a division of Bantam
Doubleday Dell Publishing Group, Inc. Its trademark, consisting of the
words "Bantam Books" and the portrayal of a rooster, is Registered in
U.S. Patent and Trademark Office and in other countries. Marca Regis-
trada. Bantam Books, 1540 Broadway, New York, New York 10036.*

PRINTED IN THE UNITED STATES OF AMERICA

OPM   0 9 8 7 6

I would like to express my special thanks to Catherine Hapka for her help in the writing of this book.

STEVIE LAKE WAS in a bad mood. She wiped her sweating brow and rested her elbows on the saddle that was sitting on the saddle rack in front of her. "I hate cleaning tack," she muttered. She glanced at her two best friends, Carole Hanson and Lisa Atwood. They didn't respond. "I said, I *hate* cleaning tack!" Stevie repeated more vehemently.

Carole and Lisa finally glanced at her, but they didn't look very sympathetic. That was because they were both busy at the same chore Stevie was complaining about, and they weren't any happier about it than she was—mainly because the temperature inside the tack room had to be at least one hundred degrees.

"Come on, Stevie," Lisa said, trying not to sound as annoyed as she felt. She was annoyed because this was at least the twentieth time in as many minutes that Stevie had stopped working to complain. "If we keep at it, we'll be finished soon."

"That's right," said Carole. "And then I'm sure Max will want us to scrub all the floors, mix the feed for the next six months . . ."

"And maybe put a fresh coat of paint on the walls while we're at it," Lisa offered, only half joking. "Actually, I forgot to tell you, Max asked me if we would muck out stalls after we're finished here." Max Regnery was the owner of Pine Hollow Stables, where the three girls took riding lessons. To keep the costs down, Max insisted that all his riders pitch in and help out with the stable chores—and there were plenty of those.

Stevie groaned and started scrubbing halfheartedly at a spot on the saddle. "It's not that I normally mind being Max's slave," she said. "But it does seem especially awful to be working so hard when it's so hot. Especially in this tiny little room. Is he trying to give us heat stroke or something?"

Lisa and Carole glanced at each other and laughed.

"Stevie, don't I recall you complaining just a few months ago that Max always seems to make you work the hardest when it's *cold* out?" Carole inquired slyly.

Stevie shrugged, but she couldn't hold back a smile, because she knew Carole was right. And then she remembered something that made her frown again. "Just think," she said, "we could be having a great time at Moose Hill right this minute, instead of hanging around here." She was referring to the summer riding camp the girls had previously attended. It held especially fond memories for Stevie because it was where she had met her boyfriend, Phil Marsten.

"We could be if it were open," Lisa corrected her. "Which it would be, if they hadn't had that wiring problem and had to close down for the rest of the month." She shrugged. "Just our luck. We had to pick the one session that got canceled."

"Don't remind me," Carole said. Stevie hadn't been the only one looking forward to riding camp this year. "As much as I love this place, I was really looking forward to getting away."

"Me, too," Lisa agreed. "Just think, we could be riding through some nice cool woods right now. . . ."

"Or swimming in the pond . . ." Carole continued.

"Or camping under the stars, in the great outdoors . . ." Lisa said wistfully.

Suddenly Stevie jumped to her feet. "Lisa, you're a genius!" she exclaimed.

"Thanks, Stevie," Lisa said with a laugh. "But why do you mention it now?"

"Because you just gave me a great idea," Stevie replied. She gestured at the tack room. "There's really no reason we should be stuck in this stuffy little room, even if we are cleaning tack. Let's move this whole operation out into the great outdoors!"

Lisa stared at Carole. Carole stared back. Then they both shrugged and smiled. "Why not?" they said in a single voice.

Within a matter of minutes the girls had dragged the tack

that still had to be cleaned and the equipment they needed to clean it out to a shady hillside near the paddock.

"I feel better already," Carole declared, seating herself on the grass with her back against the trunk of a leafy oak tree. She ran a hand through her curly black hair, lifting it off her neck. "I think I actually just felt a breeze!"

"Well, it's not Moose Hill, but it's an improvement," Stevie admitted.

Lisa nodded and picked up a snaffle bit. "Now I think it's the perfect time for a real Saddle Club meeting," she announced.

The three girls had started The Saddle Club soon after Lisa began riding at Pine Hollow. The club had only two rules: Members had to be horse crazy, and they had to be willing to help each other out. Both of those rules were easy for Stevie, Carole, and Lisa to follow. Since beginning The Saddle Club they had added a few more part-time members. One of them was Phil, Stevie's boyfriend, who lived in a town about ten miles from the girls' hometown of Willow Creek, Virginia.

Two other part-time members who lived much farther away were Kate Devine and Christine Lonetree. Kate's father had been in the Marines with Carole's father. But Frank Devine had retired a few years earlier and moved to a dude ranch out West called The Bar None Ranch. The Saddle Club had visited The Bar None several times and had become close friends with Kate as well as with Christine, whose family lived near the ranch. Since Kate had once been a champion show rider and Christine had been riding since before she could walk, they loved to talk about horses just as much as Carole, Lisa, and Stevie did. All the members of The Saddle Club—local *and* out of town—had different strengths and weaknesses as riders, so that meant they could all learn from one another all the time. And that was a big part of what The Saddle Club was all about.

Right now Lisa had a question to ask Carole. "I saw you and Starlight in the ring earlier," Lisa said. "You seemed to keep stopping him before every jump. Wasn't he behaving?"

Carole smiled. "Quite the contrary. He was behaving perfectly." Starlight was Carole's horse, a big bay gelding. She loved explaining the steps of Starlight's training to her friends almost as much as she loved working through them with the horse. Her friends liked to joke about the long-winded answers Carole gave to even the simplest questions, but usually they didn't really mind. "What I was doing was making sure Starlight knows that he's supposed to be taking his orders from me, not just doing his own thing on the course."

Lisa nodded. She knew the importance of a rider always reminding her horse who was in charge. "I'm still not quite sure how *stopping* him from jumping accomplishes that, though," she admitted.

"It's to keep him from just jumping over anything that's in front of him without waiting for the signal from me," Carole told her. "Otherwise he might start anticipating my signal and rushing the fences, which would throw off his whole performance."

Stevie, who had been riding longer than Lisa had, knew all about this aspect of training, so only half of her attention was on Carole. The other half was on a rider in the outdoor ring, which was visible from the girls' spot on the hillside. "Would you look at that," she muttered.

Lisa and Carole looked. "Polly looks like she's having fun," Carole commented. "Romeo looks great. I think Polly made a good choice." Polly Giacomin was in the same riding class as The Saddle Club. Her birthday had been a couple of weeks earlier, and her parents' gift to her had been her very own horse. Romeo was a lively brown gelding with a friendly personality that had quickly made him a favorite with everyone at Pine Hollow.

"I can't believe Polly has her own horse," Stevie said grumpily. "She hasn't even been riding as long as I have."

Lisa glanced at Stevie in surprise. It wasn't like her to be envious. "You didn't seem that upset when my parents almost bought *me* a horse," Lisa reminded her. "And I haven't been riding as long as Polly has."

Stevie shrugged. "It just seems like everyone has a horse but me these days. I mean, Carole has Starlight, obviously. Phil has Teddy. Phil's friend A.J. has Crystal. Carole's friend Cam has Duffy. Kate has Moon Glow. Christine has Arrow. Veronica diAngelo has Garnet. . . ."

"Okay, okay, we get the picture," Carole said, laughing.

"I just think it's time for me to have a horse of my own,

too," Stevie continued. "It's something I've always thought about, but lately I've been thinking about it a lot more, you know?"

"I know exactly what you mean," Carole said, and she did. She thought back to when her father had given Starlight to her. It had been one of the most wonderful moments of her entire life—the moment when she knew Starlight would be hers forever, to take care of, train, and ride. More than anything, she wished both her best friends could experience that feeling for themselves someday soon.

"I know what you mean, too, but I kind of like not having my own horse," said Lisa. "At least for now," she added quickly. She didn't want to rule out the possibility forever! "It means I get to try out lots of different horses and learn what makes all of them tick."

"Lisa's right," Carole said. "Riding all kinds of different horses can be a real learning experience. I sometimes miss that."

"Sometimes?" Stevie cocked an eyebrow at Carole.

Carole smiled. "Well, not that often, I admit it. Having my very own horse is wonderful. But there is something to be said for variety, you know."

"I know," Stevie said. "And thanks for trying to make me feel better. But I really just feel like I'm ready to have a horse of my own now."

"Have you talked to your parents about it?" Lisa asked.

"I've hinted a little," Stevie said. "But I haven't found quite the right opportunity to really mention it."

The other girls laughed. They knew what that meant. It sometimes amazed them to see the lengths to which Stevie would go to trick her parents into seeing things her way.

Carole tossed the last of the newly polished bits into the trunk, stood up, and stretched. "Come on. We'd better get this stuff back inside and start on those stalls before it gets any hotter."

Lisa stood up, too. "It's amazing how much quicker we worked once we came outside," she commented. "If only there were some way of bringing the dirty stalls out here!"

Stevie knew Lisa was joking, but she definitely agreed with the sentiment. She leaned back on the grass and groaned. "Don't tell me we actually have to go back inside now!"

"Come on, Stevie, I thought the stable was one of your favorite places in the world," Lisa teased.

Stevie didn't bother to answer. Instead she just groaned again, stood up, and began gathering up the cleaning supplies they had been using. Carole and Lisa exchanged a glance. Obviously Stevie's bad mood was back.

Soon The Saddle Club was hard at work mucking out stalls. As they worked, Stevie continued to grumble about all the people she knew who had their own horses. She was especially annoyed when she realized that the stall she was about to muck out belonged to Romeo. "Perfect," she said, shaking her head grimly. "Polly's out there having the time of her life on her very own horse, and I'm stuck in here being her stable hand."

The sound of hoofsteps on the wooden floor of the stable interrupted Stevie's stream of complaints. "That's a good boy," someone said, and the horse snorted. Carole and Lisa recognized Polly's voice.

Then Carole and Lisa recognized Stevie's voice. "Hello, Polly," Stevie was saying sweetly. "How's Romeo doing?"

"Great!" Polly replied enthusiastically.

Carole set down her pitchfork and left the stall she was working in. She was eager to see Romeo again up close.

Polly was patting the gelding's nose while she talked to Stevie. "He's really responsive—all I have to do is signal once and he does whatever I've asked," she said cheerfully. "I could never have imagined how rewarding it is to have a horse of my own!"

Carole stepped forward to pat Romeo's neck. The gelding bent his head to sniff at her, as if looking for treats. "He's a beauty, Polly," she commented appreciatively. "I know you'll love working with him—it really is rewarding to teach and learn from the same horse all the time. Starlight has taught me so much already." Then Carole's voice trailed off as she noticed the look on Stevie's face. It was a look she recognized, and it meant Stevie was hatching one of her schemes.

Carole didn't have long to wait before she found out what it was all about. "You know, Polly," Stevie said sweetly. "You're lucky you came in right now. Otherwise you would have missed out."

"Missed out on what?" asked the other girl absently. She

was much more engrossed in patting her horse than she was in listening to Stevie.

"Missed out on one of the best parts of having your very own horse!" Stevie announced dramatically.

Stevie had Polly's attention now. "Oh really? What's that?"

"The total care experience," Stevie replied. She clasped her hands together and a blissful look came over her face. Carole and Lisa exchanged a glance. They suspected what was coming. "Isn't it wonderful to think that Romeo is totally yours now? That he depends on you for every little thing?"

Stevie paused long enough to let Polly nod.

"I mean, if it weren't for you, Romeo wouldn't get fed. He wouldn't get any exercise. His tack would be a mess. His stall wouldn't be clean. What a tremendous learning experience it must be for you to be involved in every step of his care. You must really be looking forward to all that."

By this time Polly was nodding enthusiastically. "It's almost sad," Carole whispered to Lisa.

Lisa nodded. "The poor girl doesn't even see it coming," she whispered back.

Stevie was shaking her head again now. "And to think that I was about to deprive you of a major part of that joy," she said. Carole could almost swear she saw tears in Stevie's eyes. "Part of that honor. Part of that valuable learning experience." Stevie grabbed Polly by the shoulder. "Can you forgive me, Polly?"

"What are you talking about?" Polly asked, looking confused.

"I really want to make it up to you," Stevie said earnestly, ignoring the question. She picked up the pitchfork that she had leaned against the wall earlier and shoved it into the other girl's free hand. "Here you go."

"What . . . ?"

"Get ready to bolt," Lisa whispered to Carole.

"To show you how sorry I am, not only am I going to insist that you take over mucking out Romeo's stall," Stevie told Polly, "but I'm even going to let you do Comanche's and Barq's for me, too."

As the look of dawning comprehension on Polly's face turned to one of annoyance, The Saddle Club fled, trying hard not to laugh until they were well out of earshot.

A SHORT WHILE later the three girls were waiting for their ride in the driveway of Pine Hollow. They were having a sleepover at Carole's house that night, and her father, Colonel Hanson, had promised to pick them up.

As usual he was right on time, and The Saddle Club piled into the air-conditioned car with relief.

"Hi, honey," Colonel Hanson said, giving Carole a kiss on the cheek. He greeted Lisa and Stevie too. "Hot enough for you?" he inquired.

"More than," Stevie replied. "Hey, that reminds me— why did the vampire go to the tropics?"

Colonel Hanson shook his head. He and Stevie loved to trade old jokes—the older and the cornier, the better. "I give up."

Stevie grinned. "Because he liked his victims hot-blooded."

Carole groaned. "This is cruel. We're a captive audience, you know."

"We could walk the rest of the way," Lisa suggested jokingly.

"How about this one," Colonel Hanson said. "What do you call a beagle in a sauna?"

"That's easy," Stevie replied. "A hot dog."

Stevie and Colonel Hanson had time to trade a few more jokes before they reached the Hansons' house. "Finally," Carole said as her father pulled the car to a stop in the driveway. "I couldn't take much more of those jokes."

Stevie grinned. "Yeah, they're pretty good, huh?" she said innocently.

Carole rolled her eyes and pretended to be annoyed, but she was kidding and she knew that Stevie knew it, too. In reality Carole was glad that her friends got along so well with her father. Carole and her father had always been close, and they had grown even closer since Carole's mother's death a few years earlier. She would always be grateful to him for being so loving and supportive through that difficult time in both of their lives.

But today Carole was just grateful that her father had managed to joke Stevie out of her bad mood. The trick she had played on Polly had cheered up Stevie for a few minutes, but then she'd gone right back to complaining—about the heat, about not being at riding camp, about not having a horse—basically about anything she could think of, or so it seemed to Carole.

"Sweetheart, could you run and get the phone?" Colonel Hanson said as he opened the front door, snapping Carole out of her thoughts. "I can hear it ringing."

Carole obeyed, hurrying into the kitchen and grabbing the receiver off the hook. "Hello?" she said breathlessly.

"I thought you were never going to answer. I was about to hang up," said a very familiar voice on the other end of the line.

Carole gasped. "Kate!" she exclaimed happily.

"Carole, did I hear you say that's Kate on the phone?" Stevie demanded, rushing into the kitchen with Lisa and Colonel Hanson right behind her.

"Stevie, Lisa, and Dad say hello, Kate," Carole said into the phone, waving at Stevie to be quiet. "It's so good to hear from you!"

On the other end of the line, Kate Devine laughed. "I'm glad to hear that everybody's there," she said. "Just wait until you all hear why I'm calling. Then you'll *really* be glad to have heard from me!"

"HONEY, WE'RE HOME!" Stevie shouted as she stepped through the door to the main house at The Bar None Ranch two days later. Carole and Lisa were right behind her.

"Stevie! Carole! Lisa!" two excited voices shrieked. A second later the three girls found themselves smothered with hugs from Kate Devine and Christine Lonetree.

"Howdy, pardners," Carole said in her best Western accent.

"We thought you'd never get here," Kate told her.

"I can't believe we're really here now," Lisa said.

"Me, too," said Carole.

"Me, three," Stevie agreed wholeheartedly.

"Well, I for one am glad you really are," Kate assured them.

"I for two am, too," Christine said with a grin.

Stevie grinned back. "I'm just glad that businessman decided he had to make those two trips to Washington."

Frank Devine had been a pilot in the Marine Corps. Even though he was retired now, he earned extra cash by flying the private plane of a wealthy businessman named Mr. Lowell who had frequent business in Washington, D.C. Since Willow Creek was only about half an hour's drive from Washington, Frank was sometimes able to pick up Carole, Lisa, and Stevie and bring them out West for a visit. When Kate had called Carole it had been to tell her that Mr. Lowell was scheduled to make two trips East, one week apart. She wanted to know if The Saddle Club wanted to come for a visit. The Saddle Club did.

"Welcome, girls!" Phyllis Devine, Kate's mother, bustled into the room with a large plate of homemade cookies. "Come right in and sit down. We'll be eating dinner in about an hour, but I thought you needed a snack. You must be tired and hungry after your flight."

"You read my mind," Stevie told her happily.

Within a matter of minutes the five girls were settled in the comfortable lounge with the cookies and glasses of cold milk.

"Okay," Carole announced. "Let the Saddle Club meeting begin!"

"We're ready," Kate said. "What's on the agenda?"

"Horses, of course," Carole exclaimed. "What else?" Everybody laughed. Then Carole turned to Kate. "But seriously, how is Moon Glow's training going so far?"

Moon Glow was the mare Kate had adopted as part of the Adopt-a-Horse-or-Burro program run by the Bureau of Land Management. The program allowed interested people to adopt horses from the wild herds that roamed the desert. It kept the wild-horse population from getting too large for the land to support.

Kate's face lit up. "Just great," she replied. "She has such a wonderful temperament. And she's been really responsive to the training. Her foal—did I tell you I named him Felix? —is one of the smartest youngsters I've ever met. By the time he was six weeks old, he had figured out how to open the latch on the box stall where he was living. I found him wandering around, exploring the barn and making friends with everything in it."

"Sounds like a foal after my own heart," Stevie declared.

"That's right," Kate said with a grin. "He's a real trouble-maker, just like you!"

Stevie pretended to be hurt, but she couldn't do it for long. There was just too much to talk about. She turned to

Christine. "Speaking of babies, how's Dude?" Dude was Christine's puppy.

"He's doing great," Christine assured her. "But he's hardly a baby anymore. You won't even recognize him."

At that moment a group of guests wandered into the lounge, talking and gesturing wildly among themselves. Several of them were wearing brand-new cowboy hats or bolo ties, and others carried shopping bags stamped with the names of stores the girls recognized from Two Mile Creek, the closest town to the ranch.

"I wonder what they're so excited about," Stevie said curiously. "Let's eavesdrop."

It didn't take long for them to figure it out. "It sounds like they saw the show in town," Christine said with a grin. "Don't you hear that woman talking about the cowboy falling off the roof?"

"Aha! Brilliant, Watson!" Stevie exclaimed. The girls had been treated to the show Christine was referring to on their first visit to Two Mile Creek. It was a reenactment of a Wild West bank robbery and shoot-'em-up that was performed daily on the main street in town.

"It sounds like they had fun," Carole commented as she watched the guests continue through the lounge toward the dining room without even noticing the girls.

"Who wouldn't? It's a great show," Stevie said.

"I'm glad you feel that way," Kate told her. She grinned. "Because it just so happens they need some extra actors this week. Guess who volunteered. Or to be exact, guess who volunteered *you*."

Stevie, Carole, and Lisa gasped.

"You mean it?" Stevie exclaimed. "We're going to be in the show?"

"That's right," Kate said. "We're playing victims, so practice your screaming and swooning. We all get to be kidnapped by the gang of bank robbers."

"You guys really know how to entertain a guest," Lisa said. "It looks like I'm not the only one who thinks so, either," she added as another cluster of tourists hurried through the lounge in the direction of the dining room.

Kate nodded. "You're right. The ranch has been filled to capacity all summer. We had to kick a family of six from California out of your cabin. They're sleeping in the barn from now on."

For a second Lisa thought she was serious. Then she realized it was a joke, and she laughed. "Are we in our usual cabin?" she asked.

"You bet!" Kate told her.

"I'm glad the ranch is doing so well," Carole said. "I'm sure your parents are happy about that." At one point the Devines had feared they would have to close The Bar None because of competition from a nearby dude ranch.

"Oh, they're thrilled," Kate agreed. "They're especially thrilled with the way Walter and John Brightstar are working out. Remember them?"

The three girls nodded. Walter Brightstar had just been

hired as head wrangler the last time they had visited. John, his son, was a year or two older than the girls. Lisa could feel a blush creeping over her cheeks. She remembered John Brightstar especially well.

"They're both wonderful with the horses, of course," Kate said. "And John, especially, is wonderful with the guests, too. He's been leading trail rides and giving lessons, and everyone seems to love him. Not only do most of the dudes seem thrilled to be instructed by an actual full-blooded Native American Indian"—Kate paused to wink at Christine, who was also a full-blooded Native American Indian. Christine rolled her eyes in response—"but he's just so charming and knowledgeable that I think they'd love him anyway. I don't know how we ever got along without him."

"That's great," Stevie said, reaching for another cookie. "Maybe he'll entertain us with some more Native American stories, like the one he told us last time about the white stallion, and the star-crossed lovers, and—"

"Speaking of entertainment," Kate interrupted, "Christine had an idea for something to do while you're here."

Instantly the girls were all ears. They knew that Christine's plans tended to be unusual and special. "What is it?" Carole asked expectantly.

"There's an old tradition in my family that involves taking friends on long trail rides that end with a big cookout and a camp-out in the wilderness," Christine said. "I thought we could do that this week."

"That sounds wonderful," Carole said dreamily. "We'll

sleep under the stars, the way people used to in the old days of the Wild West."

"Are these camp-outs based on some sort of Indian custom?" Lisa asked.

Christine burst out laughing. "You dudes are always asking me things like that," she accused teasingly. Lisa's face turned red as she remembered the way she and her friends had gotten off on the wrong foot with Christine by assuming that, just because of her family heritage everything she did had something to do with ancient tribal customs.

When Christine saw that Lisa was truly embarrassed, she stopped laughing and apologized. "I'm just kidding," she said. "Actually, this particular tradition started because when my parents were first married, they didn't have much money. My dad was still in graduate school at the state university, and my mom was holding down two jobs to support them. They lived in a really small house, and it didn't have a guest room. So the camp-outs were a way to have guests without making them sleep on the living-room sofa."

"What a great idea," Carole said. The others nodded in agreement.

"When they moved to the house we live in now, they decided to keep doing it," Christine said. "Not because we don't have the room, but because it's so much fun."

"I can't wait," Stevie said. She finished off the last cookie on the plate and gulped down the rest of her milk. "I also can't wait for dinner. I'm starving!"

* * *

"I ALMOST FORGOT to tell you about the auction," Kate told Stevie, Carole, and Lisa as they headed into the dining room a few minutes later. "It's just about the biggest news around here right now. I was about to tell you before, but then we got distracted talking about other things, and I forgot."

"An auction?" Carole asked. "What kind?"

They all took their places around one of the dining tables, which was covered with a cheerful red-and-white-checked tablecloth.

"The best kind—a horse auction," Kate explained. "Ever since Walter and John started working here, we've had more well-trained horses than we know what to do with."

"Oh, that's wonderful," Lisa exclaimed. Then she bit her lip, wishing she hadn't said it, even though she meant it. She was afraid her friends would guess that what she thought was wonderful wasn't so much the auction itself— although that certainly sounded exciting—but rather the fact that John had something to do with it. Lisa wasn't sure she wanted them to know how much she'd been thinking about John Brightstar ever since she had arrived at The Bar None. Of course they already knew about the special friendship that had developed between Lisa and John on their last visit. But Lisa didn't know what to expect now that she would be seeing him again.

Luckily, her friends didn't seem to have noticed a thing. They were busy pumping Kate for more information about the auction.

"It's going to take place at the end of the week," she was explaining. "My mom seems determined to make it into a big event. She's going to sell a lot of baked goods and canned preserves, and she'll have sandwiches and things for sale, too."

"It sounds absolutely perfect," Carole declared.

"Good," Kate said, "because I promised Mom and Dad that you guys would help out. I hope you don't mind."

"Mind?" Stevie raised an eyebrow. "The only thing we'd mind is if you *didn't* let us help!"

"STEWBALL! YOO-HOO, STEWBALL!"

"Oh, please, Stevie," Christine scoffed. "What kind of a horse would respond to a call like that?"

"That kind of a horse," Stevie replied smugly as a horse detached itself from the small herd gathered at the other side of the corral and loped toward them. Stevie leaned over the wood-rail fence to scratch the horse, a skewbald pinto, behind the ears. "Hey there, good buddy," she said fondly. "Remember me?"

The horse nickered as if in reply.

"See?" Stevie said, delighted. "He's as happy to see me as I am to see him." Stevie and Stewball had gotten along famously since the first time they'd laid eyes on each other. Everyone thought it was because their personalities were so similar—they were both fun loving, mischievous, and a little bit headstrong.

"Well, maybe, Stevie," Kate said. "But I suspect he's also

happy to smell the sugar lumps you swiped from the kitchen."

Stevie shrugged as she fed Stewball the treat. "Believe what you like," she said airily. "I know it's because he loves me."

Meanwhile Carole and Lisa were scanning the herd for their favorite horses. "There's Chocolate," Lisa said, pointing out the dark bay mare she had ridden on past visits.

"And I see Berry over there," Carole said. Berry was a strawberry roan.

"Hey there, Eastern dudes," said a voice behind them. They turned to see John Brightstar walking toward them, a grin on his face.

"Hi, John," Carole and Stevie greeted him.

Lisa said hello, too, and gave John a shy smile. She had been expecting to see him in the dining room, but he hadn't shown up for dinner. Now here he suddenly was, which made her feel a little flustered.

"Hey, John, you should have heard Kate talking about you at dinner tonight," Stevie teased him. "She's about ready to have you knighted or something."

John laughed. "She's just buttering me up so I'll help her train that ornery mustang she's got," he teased back.

"Oh, speaking of which—where are Moon Glow and Felix?" Carole asked Kate eagerly. "I'm dying to see them."

"They're in the barn," Kate said.

"Why are you keeping them in the barn?" Carole asked. "Isn't Felix old enough to stay out with the herd yet?"

"Oh, he's old enough all right," Kate said with a laugh. "I can't remember if I explained why I named him Felix."

"I've been meaning to ask you that," Carole admitted. "It does seem like an unusual name for a horse."

"But a good name for a cat, right?" Kate said. "And you know what they say about cats and curiosity—well, Felix is about the most curious foal I ever met. Last week he decided to get curious about how a cactus would taste."

"Oh, no!" Carole exclaimed, imagining how painful the cactus prickers must have been to the foal's soft mouth. "Is he okay?"

"Oh, sure. The cactus was tiny and definitely took the worst of it," Kate assured her. "We're just keeping Felix and his mama inside for a week or two until we're sure he's completely healed." She chuckled. "He may be nosy, but he's not stupid. I don't think he'll make that mistake again. Come on, I'll introduce you to them." She stuck out her tongue at John. "Excuse us, you ornery wrangler." He just grinned in response.

The two girls headed for the barn. Stevie and Christine had gone back to leaning on the fence, talking to and about Stewball. That left Lisa alone—sort of—with John.

He smiled down at her. "Long time no see," he said.

Lisa nodded. "How have you been?" she asked lamely. She found herself noticing again how tall he was, and how a shock of his black hair fell over his forehead and one eye. She could feel her face growing warm. "It's nice to see you again," she added. The comment wasn't exactly the witty remark she would have liked it to be. But judging from the way John was smiling at her, he didn't seem to have noticed.

"Same here," he said.

Lisa searched her mind for something intelligent to say. "Kate was just telling us about the auction. It sounds like it will be a lot of fun."

John nodded. "I hope it'll be a success. In any case, it should bring in some nice publicity for the ranch."

"From what I can tell, it hardly needs it," Lisa said. "Kate told us The Bar None has been fully booked all season. And that it's partly thanks to you," she added shyly.

"A little more good publicity can't hurt," John replied. He pushed his hair out of his eyes and moved a step closer, still smiling at her. "And I'm glad to hear that the publicity about me is good these days."

Lisa was saved from figuring out how to reply to that by the return of Carole and Kate from the barn. "Lisa, Stevie, you have to see this foal!" Carole cried excitedly. "He's adorable!"

John came along to see Moon Glow and Felix, who were just as wonderful as Kate had described them, but Lisa didn't have another chance to talk to him privately. That night, as she lay in her bunk, she found herself wondering sleepily what the rest of the visit would bring. One thing she hoped it would bring was an opportunity for her and John to get to know one another even better. She had the nicest feeling that he felt the same way, and she fell asleep with a smile on her face, thinking about it.

AFTER BREAKFAST THE next morning the five girls headed into town for the rehearsal for the bank-robbery show. Christine had arrived in time for breakfast—The Bar None's usual hearty fare, which that day consisted of bacon and eggs, huge bowls of oatmeal, and grapefruit—and as soon as she and the others had wolfed down every bite, they had headed straight for the corral to saddle up.

John had been there to help them. When he heard where they were going and why, he had first burst out laughing, then let forth a barrage of teasing about the "Wild West Dude Show," as he called it. But the girls had been too excited to pay him much attention—except for Lisa. Carole had noticed her friend blushing, and she thought she knew why.

As the girls rode toward Two Mile Creek, Carole found

herself thinking about Lisa and John. She remembered how the two of them had developed a special friendship during the girls' last visit to the ranch; and she also remembered how she and Stevie hadn't had a clue about it until they were all back in Virginia and Lisa had told them. This time, Carole vowed to herself, she would keep a closer eye on Lisa and John. She didn't want to be nosy, but she also didn't want to miss whatever might happen between them.

A few minutes later they arrived in town. Two Mile Creek looked something like a town in an old Western movie and something like a regular modern town. The streets were paved, and most of the stores were the ordinary kind that might be found anywhere in the country. But the wooden sidewalks in front of the stores were covered like porches, and some of the buildings on the main street, including the sheriff's office and the bank, had hitching posts in front of them and old-West-style lettering on their signs. The girls knew that those things were mostly for the benefit of tourists—and they couldn't see a thing in the world wrong with that!

"Okay, where to?" Stevie asked, pulling Stewball to a halt in front of an ice-cream parlor.

Kate shaded her eyes with her hand and looked around. "Chuck Pierce, the guy who runs the show, said he'd meet us right here," she said. "I don't see him, though."

The others looked around, too. Suddenly Stevie pointed to a man coming out of the sheriff's office. "Could that be him?"

Kate turned to see. "That's him all right."

The man Stevie had pointed at waved to Kate and crossed the street toward them. He was wearing ornately embroidered but well-worn black cowboy boots, black pants, a black vest and shirt, and to top it all off, a black cowboy hat. He looked a little younger than Kate's father, and he had a large, bushy mustache and a heavy five o'clock shadow. The silver spurs on his boots jingled as he walked.

"Chuck not only directs the show, he also stars in it as Outlaw Buck McClanahan, head varmint," Kate explained to her friends as the man approached them.

"Howdy, Miss Kate," Chuck Pierce said in a thick Western drawl, removing his hat. "Howdy, ladies."

"Howdy," all five girls replied in one voice.

"I'm glad to see you're all in the Wild West spirit," Chuck said in a more normal voice.

"We sure are, pardner," Stevie replied enthusiastically. "When do we start?"

"Right now," Chuck told her. He put his hat back on and glanced at the horses. "Why don't you tie those critters over there." He pointed toward the hitching post in front of the sheriff's office.

"Really?" Lisa asked, glancing at Kate with raised eyebrows.

Kate nodded. "It's okay," she told them, leading her horse, Spot, across the street. The others followed. "They like to have some horses around during the show to give the place an authentic old-West look. Right, Chuck?"

"Right you are," Chuck replied as he strolled along beside them. "There's a big trough of water and plenty of shade from those trees out front, so they'll be fine there for a couple of hours while we head over to the high school for rehearsal. There's time for a quick tour of the locations you'll need to know here first, though."

After the girls had gotten their horses settled outside the sheriff's office and had loosened their girths for comfort, Chuck began the tour. He showed The Saddle Club around the area near the bank, which was two doors down from the sheriff's office. Most of the action would take place in that area. He explained that the girls would be in the first part of the show, which would take place right in front of the bank. When they were finished, the sheriff's deputy would begin shooting at the bad guys from the roof of a building across the street.

"I remember that from the last time we saw the show," Lisa remarked. "He falls off the roof, right? Kate showed us the pile of mattresses he falls onto."

"I missed that the last time," Stevie said. "Can I see?"

"Sure thing, missy," Chuck said. They followed him across the street. The shaded sidewalk ended a few yards from the street in that spot, and there was a small rest area in between, containing a park bench, a few shrubs, and a tree. Chuck led them around the bench and pointed, and the girls saw a pile of mattresses. The mattresses were hidden from view from both sidewalk and street by the shrubs and the tree.

"Awesome!" Stevie cried. "You wouldn't even know they were here!"

Kate glanced from the mattresses to the roof. "It must take some aim to hit it every time," she commented.

Chuck nodded. "We're lucky. The fellow who plays the deputy trained for a while as a stuntman before he decided he'd rather be a cowboy. He hasn't missed yet!"

"FIRST THINGS FIRST," Chuck said, leading them into the gym of Two Mile Creek High School a few minutes later. "We have to get you gals properly gussied up."

"Awesome," Stevie said. "Do we get spurs and hats like yours?"

"Not quite," Chuck said with a smile. He pointed to a tall red-haired young woman who was bustling around on the opposite side of the gym. "Go over and see Cassie, there. She'll get you outfitted."

The girls did as he said, and in a matter of moments they were dressed in their costumes for the show. Stevie was disappointed to find out that these costumes consisted of long calico dresses and bonnets that might have come straight out of *Little House on the Prairie*.

"Remember, we're supposed to be the helpless victims, not the cowboys," Carole reminded her.

But Stevie couldn't help grumbling a little, especially when she saw Cassie emerge dressed just like Chuck, with her long red hair pinned up and tucked under her black cowboy hat.

"Come on, girls," Cassie told them. "It's time to practice. Did Chuck tell you the scenario?"

The girls shook their heads. "All we know is that we're captured by bank robbers," Lisa said.

Cassie smiled. "That's right," she said. "And we're a real vicious band of desperadoes, so remember to look scared. You guys are going to be walking along innocently in front of the bank when we come out of it with our guns blazing. When we see you, each of us will grab one of you as a hostage and start dragging you toward our horses. You should all be screaming and crying out the whole time, but not so loud that the audience can't hear the rest of the dialogue."

"Then what happens?" Carole asked. When they had seen the bank-robbery show before, there hadn't been any hostages.

"While you're being carried toward the horses, one of you faints." Cassie paused and looked at each of them in turn, then pointed to Carole. "Think you can do that?"

Carole placed one hand over her forehead and pretended to swoon, crumpling dramatically to the floor. Her friends applauded the performance.

"All right, then, you win the part," Cassie said with a grin. "Another of the victims is supposed to wriggle free and run for cover." She nodded to Lisa. "That'll be you, okay?"

"Sounds good," Lisa replied.

"You"—Cassie pointed to Christine—"will wrestle the

gun away from the robber holding you and march him into the jail."

"All right!" Christine exclaimed. "I'll show those no-account varmints who's boss."

"What about Kate and me?" Stevie asked eagerly. "What do we get to do? Grab their horses and make a break for it? Knock them out with the handles of their own guns?"

Cassie shook her head. "Afraid not. You two get carried all the way over to the horses. Then they drop you, and you run for cover offstage as the shoot-out with the deputy and the sheriff's posse begins."

Carole knew Stevie was disappointed in the part she'd been assigned. But she also knew that once the rehearsal began, all of them were going to have a lot of fun putting on the performance, no matter what parts they were playing.

After the girls and the five "robbers" had practiced their part of the show several times, screams and all, everyone knew exactly what to do and when to do it.

"All right, girls," Chuck announced. "Why don't you go on and get yourselves some lunch. Just make sure you're back here by two-thirty to get back in costume. The early show is at three, and the late show is at four-thirty."

"We'll be here," Stevie assured him. "This is going to be a blast!"

"I COULDN'T EAT a thing," Stevie declared. The girls were wandering aimlessly around the town. They had already checked on their horses, who were dozing contentedly in their spot outside the sheriff's office. As the girls left them, they had noticed some tourists stopping to take pictures of the horses.

"I know what you mean," Carole said. "I'm much too excited to think about lunch."

"I'm not hungry, either," Lisa said, "but I definitely am thirsty. I've never had to do so much screaming in my life."

"Me, neither." Suddenly Stevie stopped in front of a store. "Let's go in here a minute."

"The candy store? I thought you weren't hungry," Christine said.

"I'm not." With that Stevie disappeared through the shop's door. Her friends shrugged and followed.

The candy store was decorated like an old-fashioned sweet shop, and the glass jars lining the walls seemed to contain every type of candy known to humankind. Stevie had known exactly what she wanted, though. She was already at the counter placing her order.

"Rock candy!" Lisa said as the proprietor handed Stevie a bulging paper bag. "I should have known."

"It's one of her favorite treats in the world," Carole explained to Kate and Christine.

"I don't blame her," Christine said. "It's one of mine, too. I hope you're planning to share, Stevie."

The girls left the candy shop and strolled down the covered sidewalk. "Don't worry, I'll share," Stevie said. "But this candy is mostly for medicinal purposes. I've got a little bit of a sore throat from all that screaming, and I wouldn't want to lose my voice just before our big debut." She covered her mouth with her hand and gave a weak-sounding cough.

Carole raised an eyebrow suspiciously. "You don't sound very sick to me," she said. "But as long as you stick to that promise to share, I won't say a word."

"Just don't let it spoil your appetites," Stevie warned jokingly as she held out the bag so her friends could help themselves.

"Speaking of appetites, I think we really should try to eat something before the show," Lisa said sensibly. "We probably won't have much time between the early and late shows, and we'll definitely be starving by then if all we've eaten since breakfast is rock candy."

"Lisa's right," Kate said. "Why don't we go to the hamburger place next to the ice-cream parlor? That way if anyone feels like dessert—"

"Say no more," Carole said. "Just lead the way."

THE FIVE GIRLS stepped through the doors of the high-school gym at two-thirty on the dot. Despite their excitement, each of them had managed to polish off a double-decker cheeseburger with all the trimmings and an ice-cream cone.

"I hope we still fit into our costumes," Carole commented, patting her stomach.

"I kind of hope we don't," Stevie admitted. "I'm not crazy about that silly calico dress I have to wear. I wish we had more interesting roles."

The others laughed. "Still, you have to admit this is pretty exciting," Lisa said.

"You're right," Stevie admitted without hesitation. "It is."

Chuck hurried out to meet them. "Go right on back to the locker room," he instructed them. "Cassie's waiting for you with your costumes."

The girls did as he said. They changed quickly, then gathered at the full-length mirror near the door to make last-minute adjustments.

"Is my bonnet straight?" Lisa asked anxiously, fiddling with the ribbon tied under her chin.

Carole gave the item in question a critical look, then nodded. "It's straight. Does my hair look okay?" She patted her head experimentally. She had tucked most of her curly shoulder-length hair under her bonnet, but springy little pieces kept escaping around her face.

"You look cute as a button," Kate declared. She looked around. "All of us do! Stevie, what are you doing?"

Stevie turned, looking rather guilty. She had her dress hitched up above her waist and was shoving the bag of rock candy deep into one of the pockets of her jeans, which she had left on underneath the long dress. "Oh, well, I'm kind of worried about my throat—it's sore, remember? And I'm going to have to do a lot of screaming out there, and like I said before, I wouldn't want to lose my voice at a critical moment." She held up the bag of rock candy to show them. "I thought I'd bring it along, just in case."

The others laughed. "Stevie, I'll bet you've never lost your voice in your life," Christine said. "But we might just forget you tried to use that lame excuse if you give us some more candy, right, girls?"

The others nodded. Stevie grinned and passed the bag around again. Then the five girls hurried out to join the other performers in the gym.

"Hey, where'd you get the candy?" asked one of them, a young man named Sam, when he saw what the girls were eating.

Stevie fished the bag out of her pocket once again. "Help yourself," she told the "bad guys" generously. They did. Luckily she had bought enough so that there was still some left.

"This is great," Sam declared happily as he sucked on his piece of candy. "Rock candy is my favorite."

"Mine, too," Stevie told him. "I guess that must be why we're paired up together, huh?" Sam was the one who was supposed to kidnap Stevie during the show.

"Must be," he told her with a wink. He grabbed another piece out of the bag and pocketed it. "I'll just save this for later."

"IT'S SHOW TIME," Christine whispered.

"Are you nervous?" Lisa whispered back. "I am!"

"Just pretend you're about to perform in a regular horse show instead of a Wild West shoot-'em-up," Carole suggested quietly.

"That doesn't help," Lisa replied. "I'd be nervous then, too!"

The five girls were huddled in the doorway of a jewelry store a couple of doors down from the bank. At exactly three o'clock they were supposed to stroll out and make their way slowly down the sidewalk toward the bank.

Lisa pushed back the sleeve of her dress and looked at her watch. "Okay, it's time. Let's go!"

They stepped out and began walking, trying to look

natural—or as natural as they could in their old-fashioned dresses, anyway. They saw that the bad guys' horses were lined up at the hitching post in front of the bank.

As the girls neared the bank, the sounds of gunshots came from within, and a curious crowd began to gather nearby. A moment later the bank's doors burst open and the five desperadoes backed out, holding large sacks of money and firing their six-shooters back into the bank. The girls threw up their hands and cried out in terror. Chuck whirled around and pretended to look surprised as he spotted them cowering nearby.

"Looky here, boys," he called loudly to his comrades. "I think we found us some hostages." He grabbed Kate by the shoulder. She screamed loudly and covered her face with her hands.

Stevie had to work hard not to grin as she watched. Kate looked pretty convincing—maybe she should give up riding and go into show business!

"Come here, missy," another of the bad guys shouted, grabbing Lisa by the arm. "You gals will guarantee that nobody'll try anything foolish!" He brandished his gun at the crowd to emphasize his point. The crowd gasped, loving every minute of it.

The other robbers grabbed their victims as well. As Cassie started to drag Carole toward her horse, Carole gave one final scream and then pretended to faint dead away. "What a performance," Stevie whispered to Sam, who had his gun pointed at her as he held her by one arm.

He jabbed his gun at her ribs and grimaced. "You gonna give me some more of that there rock candy, missy?" he growled in a low voice.

Stevie knew that the crowd couldn't hear a word Sam was saying. They probably thought he was uttering dire threats. She played along, letting out a few screams and then replying, "Only if you ask nicely." She almost giggled, but she knew she had to stay in character. To distract herself, she balled her hand into a fist and pretended to threaten him with it. At that he stepped forward, grabbed her around the waist, and slung her over his shoulder, just as they had rehearsed.

As he carried her along, Stevie caught an upside-down glimpse of the girls' own horses, who were still tied up down the street at the sheriff's office. While Berry, Chocolate, Spot, and Arrow looked fairly uninterested in the drama unfolding before them, Stewball had his head up and seemed to be staring right at Stevie.

But Stevie barely had time to register the fact before she was distracted by Lisa's dramatic escape. Lisa wriggled her way out of her captor's grasp and dashed down the sidewalk, almost tripping over Carole's limp form as she did so. She ran past the jail and made her escape into the sheriff's office just beyond it, shrieking all the while.

At almost the same time, Christine was wrestling the gun away from the outlaw who had grabbed her. As she got it away from him and pointed it at his head, the crowd cheered excitedly. Christine really played it up, making the robber put his hands behind his head and jabbing the gun at his back as she prodded him toward the jail. The onlookers cheered again as the two of them disappeared through the jail entrance.

Stevie watched it all with relish as she continued to scream and struggle to get away. She was having the time of her life, and she could tell the others were, too. Her only concern was for Stewball, of whom she caught glimpses every so often. He was still watching the action, and now he was snorting and stomping, seeming uneasy and restless. Stevie wondered if the gunshots were spooking him. She was a little worried, but she forced herself to put the thought out of her mind. There was nothing she could do about it right now.

"This is great!" she whispered to Sam between screams.

"Quiet, you rock-candy-eatin' varmint, you," he replied. He lifted her down, set her on her feet, and grabbed her by the shoulder. Stevie could see Kate and Chuck nearby. They were almost to the part where Chuck and Sam mounted their horses and began their escape. "Okay, now, I'm tellin' you that if you make one false move, you're dead," Sam growled to Stevie. "So if I was you, I'd let out one mighty powerful scream just about now."

Obediently, Stevie opened her mouth and let out her most bloodcurdling shriek. Just then, out of the corner of her eye, she spotted Stewball again. And this time he wasn't just watching. He whinnied and reared, snapping the lead holding him to the hitching post. He reared again and then, apparently realizing he was free, he galloped straight toward her!

STEVIE WASN'T SURE what to do as Stewball galloped toward her. Apparently Sam wasn't, either. "What's that crazy horse doing?" he whispered as he grabbed Stevie around the waist with one arm and backed quickly away from Stewball. Stevie tried to shrug in reply, but she discovered that was a difficult thing to do while being carried with both arms pinned to her side.

Stewball stopped in front of them and reared again, neighing and squealing loudly while pawing the air with his front hooves. Stevie thought he looked very dramatic. And suddenly it occurred to her what he must be doing— Stewball was trying to rescue her!

Stevie glanced around quickly. Chuck was standing beside his own horse, his gun held loosely in one hand and his other arm encircling Kate's throat. Both of them were watching Stewball, wide-eyed. Stevie glanced at Carole, who was still lying on the sidewalk. She thought she saw one of Carole's eyes open to peek at what was going on. Nobody seemed to know how to respond as Stewball finished rearing and started pawing at the ground again, snorting threateningly.

Stevie quickly came to a decision. If Stewball was determined to become a part of this performance, she was going to let him! Of course she'd have to deviate from the script, but after all, wasn't that what great acting was about—improvisation?

She wriggled out of Sam's grip. The minute she was free, Stewball stopped snorting and stood perfectly still. Sam, meanwhile, had turned to run in the opposite direction. Stevie quickly tightened the girth on Stewball's saddle, hitched up her skirt, and leaped aboard, thankful that she'd left her jeans on underneath the dress. Without any direction from her, Stewball took off after Sam. The crowd went wild.

Now Stevie couldn't stop herself from grinning just a little. She had always known Stewball had a mind of his own, but she hadn't realized just how smart he really was.

The audience continued to cheer and holler as Stewball chased Sam down the street. Sam searched desperately for someplace to hide, but every time he veered toward the sidewalk, Stewball was there before him, herding him as well as he would any recalcitrant calf. Stevie let out a whoop, and the crowd whooped back. "Go, Stewball," Stevie whispered. "You're stealing the show!"

Just then she noticed the actors playing the sheriff and his posse. They were positioned at the end of the street ready to make their entrance, looking very confused and a little annoyed. Stevie glanced up and saw the man who played the sheriff's deputy peering down from his rooftop perch across the street. She felt guilty about upstaging them right before their exciting entrance, but only for a second. She was having too much fun to worry about it for any longer than that.

Sam had reached the horses in front of the bank. He approached Spot and tried to mount him, not realizing his girth had been loosened. The big Western saddle slipped sideways under Sam's weight and dumped him back on the ground. Spot looked around as if wondering what was going on. The crowd roared with laughter, but Stevie noticed that Sam didn't look very amused. She decided he was probably just a good actor.

"Get 'im, Stewball!" she shouted, ripping off her bonnet and waving it above her head as if it were a cowboy hat. Stewball leaped forward obediently, and Sam looked around for another escape.

He headed for the stand of trees just beyond the hitching post. There weren't many trees in Two Mile Creek, since it was a desert town—just a few scattered here and there for shade. "He's lucky that isn't a cactus," Stevie remarked to Stewball as Sam shinnied up the trunk and perched on one of the lower branches.

Stewball replied by rushing up to the tree and rearing, as if trying to follow Sam up there. Stevie suspected that he looked pretty threatening to the crowd—and she could tell by the look on Sam's face that Stewball definitely looked threatening to him!

Luckily Stevie was a skilled enough rider to stay in the saddle while her horse reared. "Okay, Stewball," she said firmly, trying to calm the excited horse with her legs and her voice. "I think you made your point. We'll let the sheriff take it from here."

But Stewball paid no attention to her. He continued to rear.

"Get that beast under control, will you?" Sam hissed. Stevie thought he sounded more frightened than he should be.

"Don't worry, he won't hurt you," she called up to Sam. "He's just overexcited." She knew she was breaking character, but she decided that at this point it was necessary. She was sure that Stewball would calm down as soon as Sam did, but Sam didn't look as though he were about to calm down anytime soon.

Sam was shaking his head. "That horse is a demon. A real demon," he said. "Get him away!"

"He won't hurt you, really," Stevie repeated. "He just wants to be friends. I'm sure if you just climb down slowly . . ."

"No way!" Sam cried. "I'm not coming anywhere near that crazy horse! He'll kill me!"

From the murmurings from the crowd, Stevie could tell they agreed with Sam. She wondered desperately what she should do. Suddenly the perfect solution came to her. "Hey, Sam," she called up to him. "Do you still have that rock candy in your pocket?"

For a moment Sam looked confused. Then a look of understanding dawned on his face. He reached into his pocket, pulled out the candy, and leaned down to offer it to Stewball.

The horse sniffed, then carefully reached up and took the candy right out of Sam's hand. Munching contentedly, he backed away from the tree and stood still. Sam climbed down from the tree and cautiously stepped toward Stewball. Stewball strolled forward and began nosing Sam's pockets, begging for more candy. Stevie dismounted and gave him some of hers.

The crowd had been laughing hysterically throughout the last part of Stewball's performance, loving every minute of it. Now they burst into wild applause. Stewball turned to see what all the noise was and bobbed his head as if taking a bow. That made everyone clap even harder.

Finally Sam returned to the bank and the show continued. Stevie took Stewball back to his place with the other horses and watched from there as the performers picked up the show at the spot where Stewball had interrupted it. But somehow even the deputy's fall from the roof and the gun battle with the posse seemed like a letdown after Stevie and

Stewball's performance. The crowd applauded politely when it was all over, but it was nothing like the response Stevie and Stewball had gotten.

"Didn't I tell you, Stewball?" Stevie whispered, rubbing the horse's nose affectionately. "You really stole the show!"

6

THE GIRLS WERE not asked to repeat their performance at the late show. In fact, they were politely but firmly asked *not* to repeat it.

"Well, I for one thought you and Stewball were great," Kate told Stevie as the girls walked toward the high school to turn in their costumes.

"Stewball was pretty great, wasn't he?" Stevie said. "I always suspected he was the smartest horse I'd ever met, and now I know it for a fact. What other horse would have come galloping to my rescue that way?" She shook her head, chuckling at the memory. "I don't care if he *did* upset the show a little. He only had my best interests at heart. Besides, I thought his performance was pretty entertaining—scripted or not!"

"Me too," Carole said. "I can't understand why Chuck was so annoyed."

"I can't either," Christine agreed. "That's the best audience response that show has ever gotten. I would think he'd want to sign you and Stewball on permanently."

"Oh, well," Stevie said philosophically. "At least it means I won't have to wear this ridiculous dress any longer."

"True. And it also means we can start planning our wilderness camp-out right away," Christine pointed out.

They did just that as they reached the high school and changed back into their normal clothes. As they started back toward the main street to pick up the horses, they were deep in a discussion about whether to bring hamburgers or hot dogs to cook over their campfire. Stevie was enthusiastically supporting the idea of bringing both hamburgers *and* hot dogs when she heard a young voice shriek, "There she is! It's the funny cowboy lady!"

The girls turned to see a group of tourists approaching, led by a little girl about five years old. She rushed over to Stevie and stopped, gazing up at her with adoring eyes.

"Looks like you made yourself a fan, Stevie," Christine commented with a chuckle.

"I *loved* your show," the little girl told Stevie breathlessly. "Your horse was so funny."

"It sounds like Stewball's the one with the fan," Stevie told Christine. Then she bent down to look the little girl in the eye. "I'm glad you liked it. I'll tell Stewball—that's my horse's name—that you said so, too."

Just then the little girl's family reached them. "Sorry, I hope Susie isn't bothering you," said a young man who appeared to be Susie's father.

"She just went crazy for the show this afternoon," added the woman at his side. "When she recognized you, well, I guess she just had to meet you."

Stevie waved away the apologies with a grin. "It's no bother at all," she assured the young couple. "I just wish my horse was here to meet his fan."

"Where did you get your horse?" Susie asked. "I wish I had a horse. I want a smart, funny one just like yours, with spots and everything."

"Well, Stewball isn't really my horse," Stevie explained. "He belongs to my friend Kate's parents. But they let me ride him whenever I visit, and I love him just as much as if he were really mine. I actually live in Virginia."

"I live in California," Susie said solemnly. "But I wish I lived here, so I could watch the cowboy show every day."

Stevie chatted with her new friend for a few more minutes, until the little girl was dragged away by her parents. As The Saddle Club continued on their way, Stevie's friends began to tease her a little about her new celebrity status, but they had hardly begun before another group of tourists stopped them to congratulate Stevie on her act.

After that it seemed that Stevie could hardly take two steps before being accosted by more of her adoring fans. Carole noticed that by the third or fourth time, Stevie had stopped explaining that Stewball wasn't really her horse. In fact, Stevie started inventing some pretty tall tales about him—including one in which she and Stewball had met when he had rescued her from a pack of coyotes in the desert. Carole and the others just rolled their eyes at that one and kept quiet.

"He really is the most wonderful horse in the world," she told the group of college students who had stopped to talk to her. "I'd be happy if I never rode another horse in my life besides my Stewball."

Carole raised her eyebrows—was she imagining things, or did Stevie sound as if she had really meant that?

"Hey, you guys," Stevie said as they reached the main street. "Can we stop in the candy store again for a second?"

"Is your sweet tooth acting up again?" Carole teased. "All that rock candy you ate today wasn't enough?"

"Actually," Stevie replied, "I want to get a little bit more as a special treat for Stewball. After all, he does deserve star treatment after the way he rescued me today, don't you think?"

"You know, Stevie, now that you mention it, maybe the rock candy was the reason for the 'rescue' all along," Kate said. "He's got almost as much of a sweet tooth as you do. It's possible he was just after the sugar in your pocket this afternoon. You saw how he acted with Sam."

Stevie shook her head firmly. "No way. It's like I said before—Stewball saw that I was in danger and he wanted to help me. He probably just realized that Sam was my friend when he smelled the rock candy he had in his pocket, and that's why he calmed down."

Carole thought that sounded a little far-fetched, but she decided to keep quiet about it. After all, she wasn't entirely convinced that Kate's theory was right, either—it really had looked as though Stewball had had more than rock candy on his mind when he went after Sam.

"Well, whatever he was thinking, I think we can all agree that Stewball is quite a horse," Carole commented.

Stevie nodded her head vigorously. "That's for sure," she said. "He's my hero!" With that she opened the candy-store door and marched in to buy Stewball's reward.

"I CAN'T WAIT," Carole told her friends eagerly. "I've been dreaming for days about going on another one of those wonderful desert rides." It was the next morning and the girls were eating breakfast. As soon as they were finished, they planned to saddle up their horses for a nice long trail ride.

"Me, too," Lisa said. She nudged Stevie. "I bet you can't wait to ride your hero Stewball again either, huh?"

"Mm-hmm," Stevie murmured distractedly, stirring her oatmeal.

"Hey, Stevie, have you heard a word we've said?" Carole asked. Stevie had been quiet all morning. "Earth to Stevie!"

"I hear you," Stevie said. "I just have something on my mind, that's all. Don't worry, it's not a *bad* something," she hastened to add. "In fact, it's a downright wonderful something."

"Would you care to share that something with us?" Lisa asked dryly.

"Not just yet," Stevie replied mysteriously. "I want to wait until the time is right." She grinned and started humming a little tune.

Carole raised her eyebrows at Lisa and Kate. They shrugged, as mystified by Stevie's odd behavior as Carole was. Still, they all knew how difficult it was to pry a secret out of Stevie before she was ready to share it. Besides, they had plenty of other things to think about at the moment.

"Anyway, I can't wait to start our ride," Carole said, with one more curious glance at Stevie. "And the weather couldn't be more perfect."

Lisa nodded. "It's too bad Christine couldn't come."

"I know," Kate said. Christine and her parents were going to visit some relatives that day. Kate smiled. "But the important thing is she'll be here for the big camp-out tomorrow." The others couldn't argue with that!

WHEN THEY REACHED the barn half an hour later, John Brightstar was there to help them saddle up, as usual. "Want some help with that saddle, Lisa? It's heavy," he said, seeing her coming out of the tack room with Chocolate's bridle slung over one shoulder and her saddle in her arms.

Even though a Western saddle was larger and heavier than the Eastern ones she was used to, Lisa was perfectly capable of carrying Chocolate's saddle herself. But she knew that if she let John help her, it would give her an opportunity to talk with him some more, so she let him take the saddle from her. As she followed him out of the barn toward the corral, she thought she saw Stevie, Carole, and Kate exchange an amused glance. Her friends would probably tease her about this later on.

Lisa watched while John set the saddle on the fence and then went to bring Chocolate out of the small herd in the corral. The obedient mare gave him no trouble, and soon John and Lisa were busy saddling her up together. A moment later Carole, Kate, and Stevie joined them in the corral and began saddling up their own horses.

While Lisa and John worked on Chocolate, they talked. Lisa asked him what he had to do to get ready for the auction.

"I'm glad you asked," John replied quickly. "I was going to ask you if you'd be interested in seeing some of the preparations firsthand."

"Sure," Lisa said. "Like what?"

John leaned over to tighten Chocolate's girth. Then he straightened up and looked at Lisa over the mare's back. "I thought I'd teach you a little about cutting," he said.

"Cutting—that's like cutting specific horses out of the herd, right?" Lisa said, hoping he would be impressed that she knew what he was talking about. "It's easy to figure out from its name."

"Well, yes, you're right about what it is," John said. "Although that's actually not where the word 'cutting' comes from. A 'cut' is what the pen is called where cowboys drive the calves they separate from the herd."

"Oh, I didn't know that," Lisa said, trying to decide whether or not to feel embarrassed by her mistake. She decided not to. "I'd love to learn," she said, smiling at John across Chocolate's back.

"Great," John said, smiling back. "My father and I will be bringing in the horses early the morning of the auction. I'll give you a few lessons before then so you can help."

Lisa opened her mouth to answer, but before she could speak, she was interrupted by Stevie, who was leading Stewball past them toward the corral gate. "Hey, John, I couldn't help overhearing what you guys were talking about," she said loudly, a huge grin on her face. She glanced around at all of her friends, making sure she had their attention. "And I thought I'd better tell you that one of the horses you'll be cutting out for the auction is good old Stewball, here."

"What do you mean?" Lisa asked, annoyed that Stevie had obviously been listening to her conversation with John. "The Devines aren't selling Stewball."

Carole and Kate came over, too. "What are you saying about Stewball?" Kate asked. "I don't think my parents are planning to sell him."

"Oh, yes, they are," Stevie replied. She looked around at her friends and grinned broadly. "I wanted to wait to tell you all the big news when Stewball could be with me to hear it." She slapped the horse fondly on the neck. "*I'm* buying Stewball. Frank agreed to it—he's arranging to have him shipped to Virginia right after the auction."

"Really?" Lisa exclaimed. "You're kidding!"

"Scout's honor," Stevie replied solemnly. "I talked to my dad last night. Stewball's coming home to Pine Hollow."

"That's wonderful!" Lisa exclaimed. "Isn't that wonderful, Carole? Stewball's going to live at Pine Hollow!"

"It *is* wonderful! You're sure your parents really agreed to this, Stevie?" Carole asked, sounding excited but a tiny bit skeptical.

But John had a different question for Stevie. "What's a dude like you going to do with a cutting horse like Stewball out East?" he asked bluntly.

For a second Stevie looked taken aback. Then she put her hands on her hips and glared at John. "For your information, John Brightstar, Stewball is a *very* smart horse. He very well may be the smartest horse you or I have ever met—in fact, he's a whole lot smarter than some wranglers I could mention." She paused for breath, turning to sling one arm over Stewball's neck. "That means he's more than capable of learning anything anyone tries to teach him. I'm sure he'll make a great English riding horse."

John shrugged and turned to adjust Chocolate's stirrups. Lisa couldn't read his expression as he answered Stevie. "That's probably true," John said calmly. "He probably could learn to be an Eastern horse at that. I just wonder whether he'll like it."

"Of course he will," Stevie replied with a wave of her

hand. She was just too happy to remain angry with John for long. "He'll love it. And I know he'll especially love being with me, just like I'll love being with him. That's the most important part, right?" She looked to her friends for support.

"You're absolutely right," Carole said, nodding. "You and Stewball have a wonderful relationship. I've always thought so. You're practically made for each other."

"True," Lisa added. She looked at John. "Maybe you just haven't really seen Stevie and Stewball together enough to understand just how well they get along. I mean, you should have seen the way he rescued her from the big bad bank robbers yesterday." She giggled. "If a horse came to my rescue like that, I'd know he was definitely the horse for me —Eastern, Western, whatever."

John shrugged again. "You could be right." He gave Chocolate a pat. "She's all ready to go," he told Lisa, obviously trying to change the subject. "Let me give you a leg up."

"Thanks," she said. Carole and Kate hurried to finish with their own horses. Stevie was already aboard Stewball, leaning forward and chattering into his ears. He was listening closely—or at least that's how it looked to Lisa.

John helped Lisa into the saddle. Then, as she settled herself into the seat, he remained at Chocolate's side, looking up at Lisa. "Have a nice ride today," he told her.

She glanced down into his dark brown eyes. "Thanks," she said quietly, trying to suppress the herd of butterflies that had started fluttering in her stomach. She didn't know why just looking into his eyes made her feel nervous and flustered, but happy at the same time. She wondered if that was how Stevie felt when she looked at Phil, or how Carole felt when she looked at Cam. She hoped so. It was a nice feeling.

"Would you like to go for a walk with me after dinner?"

Lisa had almost missed John's question because she was so busy analyzing her own feelings about him. She gave an awkward gulp, then stammered out, "Oh, uh, ya—I mean yes. I mean, that would be nice."

He smiled up at her, not seeming to notice her discomfort. "Good," he said. "I'll see you then. Just meet me here by the corral, okay?" With that he turned and walked away, whistling a little tune.

Lisa watched him go, then smiled. She was a little embarrassed about her own goofy response, but that feeling was overwhelmed by a feeling of excitement. Back at home she'd been dating a boy named Bob Harris, and she liked him a lot. But John was definitely one of the most interesting boys she'd ever met, and she was looking forward to spending some time alone with him—really alone.

She clucked to Chocolate and trotted over to join her friends.

"OKAY, TIME FOR a Saddle Club meeting," Carole announced as the girls dismounted beside a small sandy stream.

They had been riding along for a little over an hour, not talking much, each of them lost in her own thoughts.

Stevie, of course, had been thinking about Stewball. The first thing she had to decide was which stall she would keep him in at Pine Hollow. After thinking over the empty stalls that were available, she decided to ask Max if she could put him in the one across from Starlight's. That was easy.

Then she had started thinking about his training. That wasn't going to be quite as easy. Stewball was such a smart horse that Stevie was sure he would be a fast learner—the only question was whether she would be a worthy teacher for him. Luckily, she knew she could count on Carole to help. After all, Carole had been working hard on Starlight's training ever since she'd gotten him. She was sure to have plenty of advice for Stevie.

Carole was thinking about much the same thing. She had already begun to outline in her mind the steps Stevie would need to take to transform Stewball from the perfect Western horse to a good Eastern one. It would be a lot of hard work, but Carole decided that with the help of The Saddle Club, Stevie would be able to do it.

Meanwhile Lisa's mind had been on a different subject entirely—John Brightstar. Even though she was having fun on the trail ride with her friends, a part of her couldn't wait for that evening after dinner. Did meeting John at the corral for a walk count as a date? After some consideration she decided that it probably did. She had just decided to share her news and her thoughts with her friends when Kate pointed out the stream and suggested they stop to give the horses a chance to rest and have a drink.

When Carole announced the Saddle Club meeting, Lisa decided this would be the perfect opportunity to talk about John. But before she could open her mouth, Stevie started chattering away.

"Did you see what Stewball did back there when that jackrabbit crossed our path?" she said. "He just lifted up his head, pricked his ears a little, and snorted. It was almost like he was telling the rabbit to get out of his way." She turned to Carole. "Did you see?"

"Yes," Carole answered. "When Berry saw the rabbit—"

But Stevie didn't let her finish. "He's not easily startled, is he?" she mused, gazing thoughtfully at Stewball. "That'll be a good quality in the show ring. He can really concentrate when he wants to, and that's important."

"It is important," Kate agreed. "I remember once when I—"

She never had a chance to finish her sentence, either. Stevie was off and running on another tangent. "I was thinking while we were riding, I'm going to ask Max if Stewball can have the stall across from Starlight's. . . ."

Lisa sighed. She had a feeling she wasn't going to be able to get so much as a word in edgewise, let alone switch the topic from horses to boys, and she couldn't help being just a little bit annoyed for a second. On the other hand, there was nothing in the world as exciting as getting your own horse, and Lisa couldn't blame Stevie for being excited. Lisa decided just to relax and join in talking about Stewball for as long as Stevie felt like it—which promised to be a good long time. Her own news could wait awhile.

She glanced at Carole, who rolled her eyes and smiled. It looked as though Carole was having the same thought.

Stevie was oblivious of her friends' silent exchange. All she could think about was Stewball. She could still hardly believe that her parents had agreed to buy him. This had to be the most exciting thing that had ever happened to her in her entire life.

She started asking Carole questions about Starlight's training. Carole did her best to answer, though most of the time Stevie was asking another question before Carole was halfway through the answer.

"Well, anyway, my main concern right now is whether to start at the beginning with his training, and how long to wait before starting on anything serious like jumping or dressage," Stevie said, interrupting Carole for about the twentieth time.

"I'm not sure, but like I started to say a minute ago, I think you might have to do at least some preliminary work with him before trying to teach him anything too advanced. What do you think, Kate?" Carole asked, turning to the more experienced girl.

Stevie glanced at Kate. She realized for the first time that Kate had hardly said a word throughout the whole discussion. "Yeah, what would you do, Kate?"

"Well, I probably wouldn't try to make an experienced Western horse into a show horse at all," Kate answered quietly. "But if I did, I guess I would start his training almost from scratch. After all, he'll need to get used to an English saddle, and to two-handed reining. That could take a little time, no matter how smart he is. You're going to be taking him away from everything he's used to and expecting him to learn a whole new way of doing things."

If she hadn't known better, Stevie would have thought that Kate didn't approve of her plan. She suddenly began to wonder how Kate felt about parting with Stewball. Even though Kate usually rode Spot, the Appaloosa she was riding today, Stevie figured she would probably miss Stewball a lot. Who wouldn't? He was quite a personality. Maybe Kate was just feeling a little bit sad. Stevie couldn't blame her for that. But she was sure that once Kate realized what a perfect match Stevie and Stewball really were, she'd know it was the right thing for them to be together all the time. Stevie vowed to prove that to Kate before Stevie and Stewball left the ranch together.

8

"THERE YOU ARE. I was wondering if you'd gotten lost on the way from the house," John greeted Lisa that evening. He jumped down from his perch on the corral fence and came forward to meet her.

"Sorry I'm late," she said. She didn't tell him the reason: She still hadn't found the right opportunity to tell her friends about her plans with him, and she hadn't wanted to spring the news on them at the last minute. That meant she had had to get away without their knowledge. To facilitate her escape, she had volunteered to help wash the dinner dishes. By the time the chore was finished, the other girls were deeply involved in a game of Monopoly, and Lisa had no problem sneaking out of the house undetected.

"That's okay," John assured her with a smile. "You're worth waiting for." Lisa and John began to stroll around the corral toward the pasture beyond. They leaned on the fence and watched the herd for a while in silence. The sun was setting, and the sky on the horizon was streaked with a dozen different shades of pink, blue, and violet. The peaceful horses were silhouetted against this breathtaking background, and Lisa thought she could watch the scene forever.

In fact, Lisa was so taken in by the beauty of the Western landscape before her that she almost forgot that John was at her side. However, when he put his arm around her, she had trouble concentrating on the scenery.

After a few minutes one of the horses broke away from the herd and started frisking around the edges. "Oh, look, it's Chocolate! Doesn't she look pretty?" Lisa exclaimed.

"Not as pretty as you," John countered.

Lisa wasn't sure quite what to say to that, so she just smiled. As she looked up at John, it seemed the most natural thing in the world that he should lean over and kiss her. It was a warm, lingering kiss, and it was nicer than Lisa had imagined a simple kiss could be.

"That was nice," Lisa whispered when it ended.

John smiled his agreement. He leaned toward her for another kiss, but before their lips met, a sharp whinny startled them apart. They looked up to see Stewball standing at the fence, staring at them quizzically.

"Oops," John said. "I think I know what he wants." He reached into the pocket of his jeans and pulled out a couple of sugar lumps. Stewball whinnied again and stretched his neck out to take them from John's palm. "I swear this crazy horse can smell sugar a mile away," John added.

Lisa laughed. "It figures," she said. "Since Stevie isn't here to interrupt us in person, Stewball decided to do it for her."

John chuckled, too, obviously remembering the times Stevie had barged in on their conversations in the past. He reached out to pat Stewball and his face grew serious. "We're really going to miss this fella around here."

"You know, I hadn't really thought of that," Lisa said. "I was just excited that Stevie is finally getting her own dream horse. But I guess you'll miss having Stewball around for roundups and that kind of thing, won't you?"

"Well, that wasn't really what I was thinking," John replied. "I just meant that we'll miss his zany sense of horse humor. There are plenty of other horses to take his place here as far as the work is concerned. In that respect The Bar None will only miss Stewball a little—but I'm afraid old Stewball will miss The Bar None a lot."

"What do you mean?" Lisa asked. "I'm sure he'll like Pine Hollow just as well once he gets used to it."

John shook his head. "I'm not so sure. I think this land and this way of life are in Stewball's blood. He belongs here in the West, at The Bar None. Stevie shouldn't be taking him to Virginia."

Lisa took a step backward. "Well, I think you're wrong," she said defensively. She couldn't believe this was the same boy who had just kissed her so tenderly. He obviously wasn't thinking about Stevie's feelings at all. "All that matters is that Stewball will have an owner who's crazy about him and will take good care of him. That's what's important."

"I was afraid you'd feel that way," John said. "But I figured it was worth mentioning to you. I was hoping to convince you to try to talk her out of it."

"You were what?" Lisa couldn't believe her ears. "Was that why you asked me to meet you here? To talk about *Stevie?*" She stared at him for a moment before whirling on her heel and storming away.

Tears came to her eyes, making it difficult for her to see where she was going. When she was sure John wasn't following her, she ducked into the barn to collect herself. The familiar smells and sounds inside were comforting, and she wiped her eyes and looked around. She felt as though she had to sort out what had just happened before facing anyone —especially her friends, who would notice right away that something was wrong.

She walked through the barn, stopping briefly to give Moon Glow and Felix a pat. Then she found an empty box stall nearby. She entered, closing the half door behind her, and sat down in the fresh clean straw, her arms around her knees. Leaning against the scratchy wood wall and taking several deep breaths, she began to think about what had just happened.

Lisa was pretty sure John had had two motives for inviting her out for a walk. One was to talk to her about Stevie and Stewball and ask her to intervene. He had more or less admitted that. His other motive had probably been just what she'd thought it was all along, namely, to be alone with her. If it hadn't, he wouldn't have said all those nice things, put his arm around her, or kissed her. She sighed, remembering that kiss. It had been so wonderful—she only wished she could just go back and tell her friends about that part and forget about the rest!

Still, she reminded herself, John had asked her to meet him only *after* he learned about Stevie's plans. That made her think that his concern about Stewball was the more important motive behind their "date," which made her feel terribly hurt and angry.

But how could he have had Stewball on his mind during that kiss? It didn't seem possible that he had been thinking about anything but her at that moment. Even if he *had* started out with another motive, did that have to make their kiss any less special? Was she being silly to think of it that way?

She sighed again and rested her head on her arms. She had a feeling this one might take some time to figure out.

"I CAN'T BELIEVE the camp-out is tomorrow," Carole exclaimed as she opened the door to the bunkhouse. Kate followed her inside. "Whoever said 'Time flies when you're having fun' was definitely right."

"You're not kidding," Kate said. "My biggest question right now is how we're going to have everything ready in time for the auction. I can't believe it's only three days away. My mom has been like a madwoman in the kitchen."

"Well, if that apple pie we had for dessert tonight was any indication, I'd say it will be worth it," Carole said. She flopped down on her bunk. "I ate so much I'll be full for three days."

"You'd better not be. Otherwise you won't be able to eat s'mores at the campfire tomorrow night," Kate teased.

"It's a good thing Stevie isn't here to hear me say this, but even the thought of s'mores doesn't tempt me right now," Carole said. Stevie had remained behind at the main house to telephone her parents and work out the details for shipping Stewball to Pine Hollow.

"Speaking of Stevie, I've been wanting to talk to you and Lisa alone," Kate began.

Carole rolled over onto her stomach and looked at Kate. Kate looked serious. "Well, since Lisa's not here, you'll have to settle for just me," she said. "Talk."

Kate took a deep breath. "I don't think Stevie should buy Stewball."

"What?" Carole sat up and stared at her friend. "Why not?"

"I just don't think they're a good match," Kate replied.

"Not a good match!" Carole sputtered. "What are you talking about? They're the perfect match. That's why she always rides him when we come out here, remember? Anyway, your father obviously disagrees with you, since he's the one who agreed to sell him to Stevie. Don't you think he knows what he's doing?"

At that moment Lisa entered the bunkhouse. "What's going on?" she asked when she saw the agitated look on Carole's face.

"Kate doesn't think Stevie and Stewball are a good match," Carole exclaimed. "She doesn't think she should buy him. Can you believe it? I mean, I know Stevie has been driving us all a little crazy by talking about Stewball all the time, but that's only natural. They're perfect for each other. Don't you think?"

Lisa sat down on the bunk next to Carole. "I'm not sure," she replied quietly.

Carole's jaw dropped. "What do you mean, you're not sure? What is everyone around here thinking?"

"If you'll give me a minute, I'll tell you what I'm thinking," Kate replied. "You didn't let me finish what I was trying to say."

Carole's mouth snapped shut and she nodded. "Sorry. Go ahead."

"When I said Stevie and Stewball weren't a good match, I wasn't talking about their personalities," Kate said. "I know they get along great. Stewball is a wonderful, responsive horse, and Stevie is a terrific rider. But the fact is, Stevie's interests and talents are in English riding. And Stewball just isn't an English riding horse."

Carole shrugged. As much as she normally respected Kate's opinion on anything having to do with horses, she remained unconvinced. "He'll learn. They've got a good relationship, and that's one of the most important things."

"True," Kate said. "But it's not the *only* important thing."

"You've said yourself that there's really not that much difference between Western and English riding," Lisa pointed out.

"That's true too, up to a point," Kate said. "There isn't anything Stewball couldn't learn and do pretty well for Stevie. The problem is that he'll be a pretty good English horse instead of an outstanding Western horse. That just seems like a waste to me."

"I don't know," Carole said. "I still think the most important thing is for Stevie to have a horse that makes her happy. Stewball makes her happy. She makes him happy. And that's the way it should be."

Kate paced the small room. Then she stopped and turned to face Carole and Lisa. "I didn't want to go into this, because you know how I feel about competition," she began.

"What?" Carole asked curiously. She and Lisa both knew that the reason Kate had dropped out of the horse-show circuit was because she didn't like the way the competition had made her forget what was fun about riding. Carole couldn't imagine what those feelings could have to do with Stevie and Stewball.

"Stevie is a fine English rider and she's getting better all the time," Kate said. "She's probably capable of going on to win plenty of ribbons. It's possible she could even make a career for herself if she wants to, especially in dressage."

Carole and Lisa nodded. Even though Stevie was impulsive and rather scatterbrained most of the time, the riding sport she was best at was dressage, which required precision and perfect concentration from both horse and rider.

"But that's not going to happen on Stewball," Kate continued. "He'll never be good enough to help Stevie compete at a high level in dressage. He's a terrific horse, but he just won't be. He'll hold her back every time. And that's not fair to either of them."

Carole thought about that for a moment before replying. She had to admit that Kate had a point. It took an exceptional horse to compete in the dressage ring. The horse had to be well trained, first of all, but it also had to have the right kind of temperament and conformation. Topside, the horse Stevie usually rode at Pine Hollow, fit all those requirements. Stewball, Carole realized now, didn't. She couldn't imagine the compact, stocky skewbald in a show ring with a bunch of tall, elegant Thoroughbreds like Topside.

She glanced up at Kate. "I guess you may be right," she admitted quietly. "Sorry I snapped at you without letting you explain."

"Don't worry about it," Kate said, waving away her apology. "The important thing is figuring out how to convince Stevie."

Lisa nodded. She had realized, belatedly, that John had been trying to tell her exactly the same thing Kate was telling them now. She also realized that they both might very well be right—and if that was true, then she definitely owed John an apology. "That's not going to be easy. You know how she is when her mind is made up. We'll have to be careful about how to approach her."

"I take it you agree, then?" Kate asked.

"I was half-convinced before I came in here," Lisa admitted. Before her friends had a chance to ask her what that meant, she offered a suggestion. "There's only one way to do it. We have to make Stevie think it's *her* idea."

"Definitely," Carole agreed. "But how?"

"Maybe the wilderness camp-out will be a good time," Kate said.

"Agreed," Carole said. "But what should we do?"

"Well, I—"

Whatever Kate had been about to say was interrupted by Stevie's arrival. Stevie came rushing into the bunkhouse, letting the door slam shut behind her. She was practically bouncing with excitement, and the words rushed out of her mouth so fast that the others had trouble following them.

"I talked to my parents," Stevie gushed. "They're such wonderful parents, did I ever mention that? Well they are. I mean I know I complain about them sometimes, but really, how many parents would buy their daughter her very own horse? Not that I don't deserve it or anything, I mean I've wanted one for ages and they did buy Chad that mountain bike which was really expensive, and Alex has his own computer and a really great stereo, but still, it's great that they just agreed to it without me even begging much at all. I think they really understood when I explained how special Stewball is and what a great opportunity it is to be able to buy him. I think Max did too—did I tell you I spoke to Max?—and I think he's excited to meet him, although of course with Max it's hard to tell. . . ."

Stevie chattered on excitedly while she started to change into her nightclothes. When she stuck her head into the bathroom to look for her hairbrush, Kate leaned over toward the others.

"Let's meet before breakfast to figure out a plan," she whispered.

Lisa and Carole nodded. Then they all settled back for another long conversation about Stewball. Only this time their hearts weren't really in it. Plan or no plan, they couldn't imagine how they were going to be able to get Stevie to change her mind about buying Stewball—without breaking her heart.

THE FOLLOWING MORNING after breakfast the girls headed toward the barn to pick up their saddles and bridles and the other equipment they would need for the camp-out. Lisa looked around as she and her friends saddled up their horses, hoping John would come out to help, but for once he was nowhere to be found. His father, Walter, was helping them instead.

"Where's John this morning?" Lisa asked him in what she hoped was a casual voice.

"He's with the herd, checking out the horses that'll be sold at the auction," Walter replied.

"Oh." Lisa was disappointed. She had hoped to have a chance to talk with John and apologize for her behavior the night before. But it looked as though that would have to wait until after the camp-out. She sighed and decided to try to put the whole incident out of her head. Instead she thought about the plan she, Carole, and Kate had come up with earlier that morning. She just hoped it would work.

"Come on, lazybones, let's get a move on!" Kate shouted playfully to Lisa. "We've got a lot of ground to cover today."

"Coming!" Lisa quickly finished getting ready. The others were already mounted and waiting outside the corral.

When Lisa had joined them, they started off across the desert to Christine's house. There they found Christine waiting on her horse, Arrow. Her dog, Dude, was with her.

When Stevie spotted the dog, she dismounted and hurried to greet him. "Dude!" she cried happily as the young dog leaped toward her and covered her face with affectionate kisses.

"He remembers you," Christine commented.

"Of course he does," Stevie said matter-of-factly. "I'm sure he also remembers that I'm the one who introduced you two." Stevie had been the one who had matched Dude with Christine after Christine's old dog had died. Stevie knew that Christine had appreciated her bringing them together —and she strongly suspected that Dude felt the same way.

They set off, with Christine in the lead and Dude frisking along beside them. As they rode, Stevie found herself thinking how absolutely perfect everything was. Not only was she having a fantastic vacation with her very best friends, but she was going to have the greatest horse in the world when she got home. She leaned forward to give Stewball a pat on the neck. Then she looked around at the gorgeous desert scenery surrounding her on all sides, and sighed in contentment.

"It doesn't get any better than this, boy," she told Stewball happily.

THEY ARRIVED AT the campsite early in the evening. Christine had led them there by what she called the "scenic route," and it had certainly been scenic. The trail had taken them across the desert, then along the edge of a deep canyon with a river roaring in the bottom of it. They had followed the canyon as it made its way toward the foothills of the mountains; then they had veered off across a pine-dotted hillside to reach a trail that led them between two steep foothills and into the valley where the campsite was located. Every inch of the trail was breathtaking. But as soon as they saw the campsite, the girls were convinced that it was the most scenic spot yet.

"This is terrific!" Carole exclaimed as she dismounted.

"Definitely," Stevie, Lisa, and Kate added in one voice.

Christine smiled. "I knew you'd think so," she said.

The campsite was in a wide, shallow arroyo that meandered through the valley. The arroyo had obviously been dry for a long time, but a clear, fast-moving stream tumbled along not far away. The valley itself was grassy and sprinkled with colorful wildflowers. On previous trips Christine's family had built a stone fire pit in the arroyo, and a temporary corral fenced with rocks and logs on the grassy plain nearby. As the valley sloped gently up to meet the surrounding hills.

the grass and flowers were replaced by a deep forest. And beyond the hills the rugged peaks of the Rocky Mountains were visible to the west.

After admiring the spectacular scenery for several more minutes, the girls unsaddled the horses and turned them loose in the corral. Then Christine demonstrated how to set up the tents they had borrowed from her parents. Dude frisked around the girls as they worked, trying to be helpful. They managed to get everything done in spite of him.

"Now what should we do?" Stevie asked when the campsite was set up. "There are a couple more hours until dark."

"I have an idea," Kate volunteered quickly. "Why don't we have an English riding demonstration? Christine was asking me just the other day what English riding is all about."

"What? I mean, oh yeah," Christine said. "That would be cool."

"Oh, yes!" Carole chirped. "It will be *so* much fun!"

"Definitely!" Lisa added enthusiastically.

Stevie shrugged. "Okay, that sounds like fun, I guess." She glanced at Stewball and grinned. "Actually, it will be terrific. This will be my first chance to see how Stewball takes to English riding. I know he'll be a natural!"

As she hurried over to the temporary corral, Stevie didn't notice the triumphant look that passed among her friends.

STEVIE GREW MORE worried by the second as she watched Kate and Carole put their horses through some basic dressage moves. Or, rather, as she watched Kate and Carole *try* to put their horses through some basic dressage moves.

Kate went first. Spot fought her tight rein the whole way, shaking his head and skittering sideways nervously every few steps. Kate gave up after only a few minutes.

Carole went next. Berry didn't fight her, but he seemed confused about what he was being asked to do. Every few minutes he drifted to a stop and looked around, as if pondering what purpose there could be in trotting back and forth from one point to another.

Stevie was becoming more and more worried that Stewball wouldn't catch on to dressage either. In fact, that tiny worry had been nagging at her since soon after she had decided to buy Stewball. She knew he was a Western horse born and bred, and she had been so excited at the thought of owning him that she hadn't really thought about whether it was practical to try to convert him to a whole new way of doing things. No matter how much she wanted to be with him, was it fair to ask that of him?

After watching her friends' disastrous attempts, Lisa didn't even want to give it a try. Stevie wasn't sure she wanted to, either, but she knew she had to. She had to know whether Stewball could do it. Her heart was in her throat as she mounted Stewball and aimed him toward the far corner of the "dressage arena" they'd marked off in the field. Taking a deep breath, she signaled for a slow trot and began to put him through an exercise she had been working on at home with Topside.

At first Stewball seemed a little perplexed by all the orders his rider was giving him. Stevie knew he had a mind of his own—and she knew that if he got it into that mind that he didn't want to do dressage, there would be no changing it. But after a few minutes he settled down and began to respond to her commands as best he could.

Stevie felt a hundred percent better when they had finished the exercise. As she brought Stewball to a four-footed stop in the middle of the arena, she was grinning from ear to ear. "I knew he'd be a natural!" she crowed. Though Stevie would be the first to admit that Stewball was no Topside, the Western horse had caught on fast and done a creditable job in the end. Remembering how she had wanted to prove to Kate that Stewball could make it as an English horse, Stevie was sure she had just met that goal. And more important, she had convinced herself.

She dismounted and led Stewball over to where the others were sitting at the edge of the field. "Could you tell what was going on?" she asked Christine.

"Oh, yes," Christine said. "Carole and Kate explained everything to me."

"Good." Stevie grinned at her friends and was a little surprised when they didn't grin back. In fact, they looked rather distracted. She shrugged and decided they were probably just overcome with admiration for Stewball's talents. "Obviously Stewball isn't an expert, and it's better if it's done exactly right. But he did well enough to give you an idea. And before long he'll be an old pro! After all, dressage isn't really that different from cutting when you think about it."

Kate raised her eyebrows skeptically. "Oh, really? How do you figure?"

"When he's cutting a horse or a calf out of a herd, Stewball has to be constantly on his toes, ready to change directions at the drop of a hat," Stevie said. "In dressage a horse has to be ready to follow his rider's instructions instantly, whether it's to change leads or lengthen his gait or whatever."

"I guess that makes sense, as far as it goes," Kate agreed cautiously. "But, remember, a cutting horse does all that stuff on his own. A rider shouldn't have to give his cutting horse any instructions at all aside from which calf or horse he wants him to cut out of the herd. In fact, in a cutting competition you can have points knocked off if the judges see you giving your horse obvious instructions."

"That's very different from dressage, then," Carole commented. "In dressage a horse has to always be prepared to do exactly what the rider says, no questions asked."

"I know all that," Stevie said impatiently, a little annoyed that Carole and Kate seemed to find it necessary to lecture her on dressage. "I just meant that Stewball has the natural ability to do it. He hasn't been trained yet, so obviously he's not going to get it perfect the first time out. But he did a lot better than either of the other horses, and I think that says something about his abilities." She turned to Christine. "So do you want to see more?"

"Uh, no," Kate broke in. "Christine's probably tired of dressage. Let's show her something more exciting. How about some jumping? It won't be easy in a Western saddle, but we can make the jumps low."

"Sounds good to me," Stevie agreed breezily.

A few minutes later the girls had finished constructing a jumping course in the field. They had stacked rocks and tree branches to make obstacles about eighteen inches high.

"Who wants to go first?" Kate asked.

"I'll try it," Lisa volunteered. She started Chocolate on the course at a trot, but it was clear from the beginning that the mare was confused about what she was being asked to do. She veered around almost every obstacle despite Lisa's best attempts to keep her on track. The few times Lisa managed to keep Chocolate going, the mare slowed to a walk and stepped carefully over the logs.

Finally Lisa gave up and brought Chocolate back in. "I guess she's just not cut out to be a jumper," she said, dismounting.

"That's okay," Kate said, giving the mare a pat on the rump. "She has other skills. Anyway, who would expect a Western horse to do Eastern horse tricks?"

"Why don't you and Spot give it a try, Kate?" Carole suggested. "You're such an experienced rider that you should be able to make it through the course on a Western horse if anybody can."

Kate and Spot did better than Lisa and Chocolate had, but not by much. Before every obstacle Spot started shaking his head anxiously and trying to change course. Kate's firm hand and expert riding eventually got the horse over all the jumps, but he didn't look happy about it.

"I guess Spot has that Western horse mentality," Kate commented when she rejoined the others. "It's not that he *can't* jump those obstacles. He just doesn't see the point."

"And by his age I bet he's pretty stuck in his ways," Lisa said with a nod.

"He probably is, even though he's not really that old," Kate said. "I mean, he's a year or two younger than Stewball, for instance."

Stevie couldn't understand why her friends were being so downbeat about this whole demonstration. It wasn't like them. "Lighten up, you guys, this is just for fun," she told them. "Anyway, I'll bet Stewball can do it. He'll show these other horses how it's done."

Carole shrugged. "Well, if you want to give it a try . . ."

"Come on, boy, let's go," Stevie said to Stewball as she mounted. She signaled him to trot and aimed him at the first jump. His ears flicked forward, and as he approached the obstacle, he hesitated for just a moment. But at Stevie's urging he picked up his pace again and took the jump perfectly. After that he seemed to understand what was going on. He cleared the course easily.

When they had finished, Stevie slowed Stewball to a walk and leaned forward in the saddle to give him a big hug. "You were terrific, Stewball!" she exclaimed. Any doubts she had had about teaching Stewball English riding skills had vanished. She had been right in the first place. He was the smartest horse in the world, and he could learn anything.

SOON IT BEGAN to grow dark. The girls unsaddled and groomed the horses, then set them loose again in the makeshift corral. Together The Saddle Club began gathering dry sticks and twigs from the area around the campsite. It didn't take them long to find enough, even with Dude running around and getting in their way.

"I guess that's one advantage of this dry climate," Lisa commented. "Back home in Virginia it's usually a lot damper, so a lot of the wood you find is too damp to use."

Christine wasn't listening. "Look at that," she said.

The others turned and saw what she was looking at. The sun was setting, throwing off streaks of deep red, orange, and violet. Carole, for one, was sure she had never seen such a beautiful sunset. "This place is different from home in a lot of ways," she commented quietly.

The girls watched the sunset until it began to fade, then finished their task. Before long a campfire was crackling merrily in the fire pit. The girls settled down to roast their hot dogs (they had finally decided against bringing hamburgers, too) and to talk.

"This is so much fun," Lisa said. "I'm glad you suggested it, Christine."

Christine leaned back against a boulder and gazed up at

the sky, where the stars were growing brighter as the last bits of daylight faded. "I love it out here," she said. "It's so peaceful and free. Just us and nature." She took a hot dog out of the package and tossed it to Dude, who gulped it down and wagged his tail gratefully.

"It's like we're a million miles away from everything," Carole agreed.

"Yup," Kate said. "Just us and our horses."

"Speaking of horses," Stevie began. Carole noticed that Stevie seemed to be the only one not affected by the quiet, reflective mood. "Can you believe Stewball? I mean, I have to admit I was a little worried about how he'd take to English riding, but now I can see there'll be no problem. He's just brilliant, isn't he?"

"Brilliant," Kate replied. Carole was pretty sure Stevie didn't notice the sarcasm in Kate's voice.

"I know," Stevie said dreamily. "He really can do anything. He's the perfect horse."

The others exchanged glances. Carole was pretty sure she could see her own thoughts reflected on her friends' faces. Maybe they had been wrong about Stewball. He really had performed very well in the English riding demonstration despite his complete lack of training. If he learned that fast, who could say that he wouldn't make a fine show horse someday, especially with such a devoted and loving owner? And more important, who could say he wouldn't be happy doing it?

Carole sighed and finished the last bite of her hot dog. "I'm beat," she said. "Let's hit the sack."

"Sounds good to me," said Kate, stifling a yawn. "It's been a long and interesting day."

Carole had a feeling Kate wasn't talking about just the ride.

When Stevie awoke, it took her a moment to remember where she was. It was pitch-black. The sound of light snoring came from nearby.

Then she remembered. She was in a tent in a Western arroyo. The snoring was coming from Carole. Stevie yawned, wondering what had awakened her. Carefully, so as not to disturb her friend, she pulled Carole's arm out of her sleeping bag and pressed the button on her light-up digital watch. It was well past midnight.

Stevie let Carole's arm drop and sat up. Carole moaned and rolled over but didn't awaken. Then Stevie heard noises outside coming from the direction of the corral. Her heart began to pound. What if some kind of predator was threatening the horses? She crawled to the entrance of the tent and peeked out. The entire area was bathed in moonlight, giving the landscape a luminous white glow as if it were covered by a thin layer of snow. It was beautiful, but eerie at the same time.

Then Stevie saw Dude dozing by the remains of the campfire, and she relaxed. If there were any dangerous animals around, she was sure the dog would have scented them and sounded the alarm. But, then, what were the horses doing? Judging by the noise they were making, they were restless, but Stevie couldn't see them from the tent.

Just then a whinny came from the corral. "Stewball," Stevie whispered. Trying to be as quiet as possible, she crawled back into the tent and felt around in the dark until she found her boots. She pulled them on and slipped out of the tent.

Outside, she stood up and looked around, marveling at how different everything looked in the moonlight. Dude had awakened as soon as she came out. He looked up at her and seemed to grin, his tail thumping on the ground. When Stevie headed toward the corral, the dog jumped to his feet and followed.

"Let's just see what that crazy Stewball is doing now, huh, boy?" Stevie whispered, bending down to scratch behind Dude's ears. As they walked past Christine's tent and then the one Lisa and Kate were sharing, Stevie could see that the horses were milling around in the corral.

When she got closer, Stevie realized they were playing. She sat down on a boulder near the fence to watch, hoping they wouldn't notice her presence. She held Dude beside her, and the dog sank to his haunches, seeming to understand the need for quiet.

Stevie could tell right away that Stewball was leading the game. The silvery moonlight made the white patches on his coat glow brightly as he raced around, dodging in and out among the other horses. Stevie couldn't tell what he was doing, but he seemed to be having fun. After watching a little longer she decided that the horses were playing some version of tag, though she couldn't begin to figure out the rules.

Berry let out a nicker and chased after Stewball. But Stewball was too fast for him—he darted from side to side, changing directions so quickly Stevie could hardly believe it. Then he doubled back and dodged behind Spot, who was watching the action with his head held high. Spot tossed his head, snorted, and set out after Berry, who whirled and raced away. Chocolate joined in too, and soon all five horses were involved in the game. Stevie watched breathlessly, feeling she was witnessing something few people ever got the chance to see.

Finally it all seemed to be over. Stewball raised his head and neighed, stomping his feet as if in triumph. Stevie grinned proudly. She wasn't positive, but she had a hunch that whatever the game had been, Stewball had won. He led the other horses on a slow lope around the field, stopping at the far end, where he paused on a small hillock to shake his head and neigh again. The sound drifted back to Stevie through the still night air, and she shivered. For a second the horse poised there, framed against the dark, wild back-drop of the mountains, seemed alien from the Stewball she knew. At that moment he seemed only one small step re-moved from the wild herds she had seen out here—the bands of horses that roamed the rugged Western land, never knowing the feel of a saddle on their backs or the touch of a human hand. She shivered again and blinked, and then he was just Stewball again as he lowered his head and ambled off in search of a tasty patch of grass.

As the horses settled down, Stevie got up and headed back to her tent. She wrapped her arms around herself, realizing for the first time how chilly it was. After patting Dude good night she crawled inside. Carole hadn't moved, although Stevie was happy to notice that she had stopped snoring.

Snuggled back inside her warm sleeping bag, Stevie closed her eyes and waited for sleep to come. But her mind was still wide awake, filled with images of the beautiful scene she had just witnessed. As if she were still there, she saw the horses frolicking in the moonlight, absorbed in a game only they could understand. They had looked so free and happy under the huge canopy of stars. And Stewball had seemed the happiest of them all as he led them in the game, obviously in his element and having the time of his life.

It took Stevie a long time to fall back to sleep.

* * *

"COME ON, YOU lazy dudes! Rise and shine!"

Carole opened one eye and groaned. "Is it morning already?" she muttered sleepily.

"I guess so," Stevie said with a yawn. She sat up and stretched, then flopped back down again. "I say we go on strike."

Christine's head poked through the tent flap. "Come on, you two, up and at 'em," she said cheerfully. "I've been up for hours already—the day's half-wasted!"

Carole glanced at her watch. "Only you would say that at six in the morning," she commented. It was true. Christine was known for her predawn rides through the desert.

"Up, up, up," Christine replied with a grin. "I already took care of the horses, and our breakfast is almost ready."

Reluctantly Carole and Stevie left their cozy sleeping bags and pulled on some clothes. When they got outside, they discovered that Christine had the campfire going, and slabs of bacon were sizzling in a cast-iron pan.

"Where did you get that pan?" Lisa asked as she and Kate came crawling out of their tent, yawning and stretching and looking as sleepy as Carole and Stevie felt. "I didn't know you brought it."

"I didn't," Christine said. "I got it from my family's secret hiding place." She led the others to a small opening in the rocks at the edge of the arroyo, too small to be called a cave. Inside was a large, sturdy wooden trunk bound in metal. Christine opened the lid and showed her friends the contents: cooking and serving utensils, extra drop cloths and blankets, a spare halter and lead rope, clothes, and packets of dried food.

"Wow," Stevie said, impressed. "Nobody would ever know this stuff was here if they didn't know where to look."

"My family has been coming to this spot for a long time," Christine said. "This way we don't have to carry absolutely everything with us every time, and we're prepared in case of emergencies."

She grabbed some plates and forks out of the trunk. Then the girls returned to the campfire and helped themselves to bacon and slices of Phyllis Devine's homemade bread, which Christine had toasted over the fire. Of course, Christine gave Dude his share of everything.

"This is delicious," Carole murmured, her mouth full.

"Somehow I always think food tastes better when it's prepared outside," Christine commented.

Lisa nodded. "I know what you mean, especially when it's eaten outside as well." By this time the girls were all wide awake, and within a few minutes they had finished every last bit of the delicious breakfast.

"I guess we'd better think about cleaning up and heading back soon," Kate said reluctantly. "There's a lot of work to be done before the auction tomorrow."

"Before we do, I have one last surprise for you," Christine said mysteriously. "Come this way." She stood up. "Oh, but first you'll need to change into your swimsuits. I hope you brought them like I told you to."

"I have a feeling I'm going to like this surprise," Stevie

remarked to Carole as they returned to their tent and hurriedly changed into their suits.

When everyone was ready, Christine led them up the far bank of the arroyo and through the woods beyond the corral. There they joined a creek—the same one that meandered past their campsite, Christine told them. They followed the creek through the woods until it flowed over a small drop-off and emptied into a peaceful, shady pond nestled among the trees.

"Oh, it's beautiful!" Lisa exclaimed. Just enough sunlight filtered through the treetops to set the calm surface of the water sparkling.

"The shade keeps the water cool even during the heat of the day," Christine explained as she stepped down past the small waterfall onto some large, smooth rocks along the edge of the water below. She shed her T-shirt, boots, and socks, then slid into the water. "Come on in!" she urged the others.

They didn't have to be asked twice. Soon all five of them were happily splashing around in the pond. The water came up only to their shoulders, so it was too shallow for diving, but plenty deep enough to have fun swimming and dunking each other. "I thought there was supposed to be hardly any water in the desert," Stevie said after a few minutes. She kicked her feet up and floated on her back, gazing up into the treetops above.

"That creek is fed by a natural spring in the mountains," Christine explained. "Even during the driest times this pond is always at least partially full. That's one reason my parents chose this particular campsite."

"Well, I for one am glad they did," Carole announced. She ducked her head under the water and smoothed back her hair, then hauled herself out of the water onto one of the flat rocks and settled back contentedly to let herself dry off.

"Me, too," Stevie, Lisa, and Kate agreed in one voice.

After a few more minutes the girls put their boots back on and returned to the campsite. They all wished they could stay longer, but there was work to be done for the auction, and they knew that would be fun, too. Besides, Carole told herself, as long as the Devines owned The Bar None—and she was sure they would for a long time to come—The Saddle Club would always be welcome at the ranch. There were sure to be more trips West, and more camp-outs like this one. And that was a very nice thing to think about indeed.

12

CAROLE, STEVIE, LISA, and Kate arrived back at the ranch a couple of hours before lunchtime. They had ridden straight home from the campsite, dropping Christine off at her own house, though she promised to come over to The Bar None later in the day to help out. Walter came out of the barn as the girls rode up to the corral.

"Whoa, there," he called to them with the hint of a smile. "Y'all are looking kinda trail weary."

"Us? No way," Stevie replied tartly. "What do you think we are, a bunch of dudes?" Still, she didn't object when Walter offered to take care of the horses while the girls got cleaned up.

After a shower and a quick snack, the girls were completely refreshed and ready to get to work. And there was plenty of work to do, just as Kate had promised. Frank put

Stevie and Kate on whitewash duty. Their task was to make sure the fence around the corral looked its very best for the auction. Meanwhile Phyllis had asked Carole to help her in the kitchen, where she was busy making huge vats of lemonade and piles of homemade cookies. Carole was happy to join right in, especially after tasting a few of the cookies.

Lisa decided this would be a good time to find John and apologize. She had managed to put him out of her mind during the camp-out, but now she found herself thinking about him again. She told Phyllis and Carole she wanted to ride out and see if John needed any help—leaving out the part about the apology—and accepted the brown-bag lunch Phyllis quickly put together for her. Then Lisa checked with Walter and found out that, as she had expected, John was out on the range working with the herd.

A few minutes later Lisa had Chocolate saddled up and was on her way to find him. It didn't take long; the herd was grazing not far from the ranch, near a stand of trees that Lisa knew from previous visits hid a small water hole. As always Lisa was impressed by the size of the herd. It wasn't often that she had an opportunity to observe seventy or eighty horses together on the open range.

Today, however, she had other things on her mind. She looked around and soon spotted John nearby, astride a buckskin horse named Peanuts. He was sitting still, watching the herd with a thoughtful look on his face. As Lisa rode up to him, he turned and smiled at her.

"Hi, there," he said. "I was just thinking I could use a hand, and here you are."

"Hi, John," Lisa replied, shyly returning his smile. "I wanted to find you and apologize about the other night."

"Accepted," John said with a wave of his hand. "Now, will you help me? I want to make sure exactly which horses we'll need to cut out tomorrow morning."

"Okay," Lisa said uncertainly. "But I really wanted to explain about the things I said. . . ."

"Later, okay?" John smiled at her again and then went back to scanning the herd.

Lisa had the feeling he wasn't really listening to her, but she thought she knew why. He was anxious about the auction and wanted to make sure everything went smoothly. She could understand that, so she decided a more detailed apology could wait awhile. "Sure. What do you want me to do?"

"We don't need to actually cut the horses out yet," John explained. "We'll do that first thing tomorrow morning. Right now, though, I want a chance to watch each horse in motion so we'll know what we've got. That'll make things easier tomorrow."

"Sounds good," Lisa said. "What's my job?"

"You're going to get your first cutting lesson," John said. "I'll tell you which horse I want to see, and you and Chocolate will go get it and put it through its paces."

"All right," Lisa said doubtfully. "But I just have one question."

"What?"

"How do I do that?"

John laughed. "Don't worry, it's really not hard, especially with this herd. Most of the horses are pretty well trained and aren't likely to give you much trouble. And Chocolate there is a pro—she'll do most of the work. All you really have to do is tell her which horse to go after, and what she should do with it once it's out."

Lisa shrugged. "Well, okay," she said, still sounding dubious. "Let's give it a try."

John pointed out a bay mare grazing at the near edge of the herd. "Why don't you start with Ellie there?"

"Okay, here goes nothing." Lisa signaled Chocolate into a walk and aimed her at the mare. Chocolate's ears pricked forward eagerly and she set to work. John had been right. Chocolate knew exactly what she was doing. Within minutes she had managed to get the mare, who seemed reluctant to leave the patch of grass she had been munching on, out and away from the rest of the herd. The other horses hardly seemed to notice.

"Great!" John called, trotting toward them. "Now put her through her paces."

Lisa assumed she wasn't going to get much instruction on how to do that, either, so she decided to figure it out herself. Both Chocolate and Ellie had come to a stop. Lisa nudged Chocolate with her heel, and again the mare seemed to know exactly what her rider wanted. She in turn nudged the other mare until Ellie was walking.

"Now, how do I get her to trot?" Lisa muttered to herself. She signaled Chocolate to trot; then, when she was close enough, she leaned over and gave Ellie a healthy smack on the rump. Startled, the mare broke into a trot. Chocolate followed. When she drew abreast of the other horse, Lisa signaled for a canter—or a lope, as it was called out West. Ellie broke into a lope as well, although after a minute she seemed to wonder what she was doing and quickly slowed to a walk. Lisa turned Chocolate aside and let Ellie amble back to the herd.

"Good work," John told Lisa as she trotted over. "We'll make a wrangler out of you yet."

Lisa grinned, pleased by the compliment. "Who do you want to see next?"

For the next couple of hours John kept Lisa and Chocolate working hard. By the time he finally seemed satisfied, Lisa's stomach was growling. "Hey, I know us cowpokes are supposed to be hardy and everything, but does that mean we have to skip lunch?"

John glanced at his watch in surprise. "Wow, I didn't even notice how late it was getting," he exclaimed. "Sorry about that! Tell you what, I'll make it up to you by showing you my favorite picnic spot. Come this way."

He led her toward the trees. Dismounting, he loosened Peanuts's girth and led him to the water hole. Lisa did the same with Chocolate. After the horses had had a drink, John and Lisa left them ground-tied nearby while they settled down to eat.

The spot John had selected—a small shady clearing among the trees, with a view of the water hole and the meadow beyond—*was* pretty, Lisa thought, and she told him so. "But I think I'm getting spoiled," she said, thinking of Christine's campsite. "There are so many beautiful spots around here."

"It's a beautiful land," John said, biting into a peanut-butter sandwich. "I don't think I could live anywhere else."

"That sort of reminds me," Lisa said with a gulp. "I really do want to apologize for the way I acted the other night—you know, when you said you didn't think Stevie should buy Stewball."

John shrugged. "That's all right," he said. "You had a right to be upset. It's really not my business what Frank and Stevie decide to do as far as Stewball's concerned."

"I realized later that what you were saying made a lot of sense," Lisa said. "But when you said it, I just automatically jumped to Stevie's defense without thinking about it."

"That just shows you're a good friend," he replied. "I understand."

"Good," Lisa said, feeling relieved. "So you're not mad at me for running off like that?"

"Not at all," John said. "To tell you the truth, I never was mad, just worried. I thought I'd hurt your feelings, or maybe frightened you—after all, I am a couple of years older than you are. I was sure I'd really messed up."

"I didn't think of it that way," Lisa said. "Anyway, people are always telling me how mature I am for my age."

"Yes, but what they usually mean is that you get good grades and stuff," John said. "Not that you're any wiser or more experienced than other people your age."

Lisa shrugged. "I guess you're right." She wondered if that meant he thought she was a baby. To make sure he didn't, she decided to take the initiative—she leaned over and kissed him.

He seemed surprised but pleased, and he kissed her back. But after a moment they heard noises coming from the herd. John broke away and looked down the hill. "I wonder what's wrong with the horses?" he said.

"I don't know," Lisa replied, a little breathless from the kiss, which had been just as wonderful as the first one.

"They seem edgy," John said. He frowned. "I really hate to say it, but I think we should get down there and get them away from here. There might be a predator hanging around the water hole."

He stood up and reached down to help Lisa to her feet. They quickly gathered up the remains of their lunch and hurried to the spot where they had left Chocolate and Peanuts. The two horses were well trained and so were right where they had left them, but they were obviously nervous. Lisa and John tightened the girths on their saddles, mounted, and rode toward the herd.

"It's a good thing we were here," John said, glancing back at the stand of trees surrounding the water hole. "From the way the horses are acting, I have a strong feeling there's a visitor lurking back there that likes horses—for lunch."

Lisa shuddered at the thought. She wondered if the predator liked people for lunch, too. But she didn't have long to think about that. She and John had work to do.

LUCKILY THE HORSES were nervous enough about whatever they had sensed nearby that they were willing to abandon the water hole and the tasty grass without much prodding. John and Lisa herded them in the direction of the ranch and managed to keep them moving until they were a safe distance from the stand of trees and whatever might be hiding there. By that time the house and barn were within sight.

"I guess we should just head back," John said, wiping his brow and gazing out over the herd. The horses had already settled down to their grazing again, the danger past. "It's almost dinnertime, and besides, I'm beat."

"Me, too," Lisa agreed quickly, and she meant it. Their kiss seemed like a pleasant but distant memory now after the hard work of herding. "I guess it will be an early night for everyone," she added.

"I guess so," John said. He glanced at her. "I hope you're still planning to come along tomorrow morning to bring in the horses for the auction."

"I wouldn't miss it for the world," Lisa assured him. And she definitely meant that, too.

By DAWN THE next day everyone at The Bar None was up and busy. Carole and Kate headed into the kitchen to help Phyllis finish the food preparation while Stevie and Lisa rode out with Frank, Walter, and John to bring in the horses.

"Stewball sure is antsy this morning," Stevie remarked as she mounted. He hadn't seemed able to hold still while she was saddling him up.

"I guess he didn't like spending the night in the corral," John said. To save time, John and Walter had left Stewball and the other four horses in the corral instead of turning them out with the herd as usual.

Stevie laughed as Stewball tossed his head and snorted. "Well, at least he's got plenty of energy for the work he's about to do."

It didn't take the riders long to find the herd; it was still more or less where John and Lisa had left it the evening before.

"Good," Frank commented. "That makes things easier. Once the horses we want are separated, we won't have far to bring them."

"Let's get to work," Walter said. He squinted at the herd. "You checked them over yesterday, didn't you, John?"

John nodded and rode over to join the two men. As they discussed which horses would be auctioned off, Stevie and Lisa watched the herd.

"They sure look peaceful, don't they?" Lisa commented.

Before Stevie could answer, John came riding over. "Time to quit yapping and start working," he told them.

"Just tell us what to do," Stevie said.

"Well, for starters you could head off that black gelding who's trying to sneak away," John said, pointing. "He must have heard he was going to be sold."

The girls looked where he was pointing and laughed. "He does look like he's trying to sneak away without being noticed," Lisa said. While most of the other horses were grazing calmly, this particular horse, a black quarter horse gelding with three white feet, seemed to be sidling away on the outskirts of the herd.

Frank rode over and noticed where they were looking. He grinned. "That's Midnight. I don't know where he thinks he's going, but I guess someone had better stop him."

"Leave him to me and Stewball," Stevie declared. She sent Stewball toward the black gelding.

Stewball's ears perked forward as they approached the herd, and he seemed to know exactly what was expected of him. The black gelding tried to avoid him, backing away and then quickly dodging behind a nearby mare. Before Stevie could make any sort of signal, Stewball responded. Quick as a wink he was behind Midnight, nudging him forward. Midnight took a few steps in the direction Stewball wanted him to go, then whirled and raced away from the herd in the opposite direction. Stewball followed. A second later he caught, passed, and cut off Midnight. The black gelding continued to resist for a few more minutes; in fact, Stevie would have sworn he was actually having fun doing it. But finally he seemed to realize he was no match for Stewball, and he gave up. Soon he was ambling obediently ahead of Stewball.

"Wasn't Stewball great?" Stevie exclaimed breathlessly as they approached the others. "He did all the work—all I had to do was hold on!"

"He was terrific," Lisa said sincerely. If she had thought Chocolate was good the day before, Stewball had just demonstrated that he was even faster and more skilled.

"I have a feeling Midnight here was one of our toughest customers," John said. "He's almost as much of a trouble-maker as . . . well, Stewball!"

The others laughed. Then they got back to work. Walter pointed out two more horses, and Stevie and John went to get them. As they brought them over to join Midnight, Lisa and Walter took over, keeping the new, smaller group of horses separate from the main herd.

Stevie was enjoying herself immensely. It seemed that all she had to do was point Stewball at a horse and he took care of the rest. John had been right; most of the horses put up far less resistance than Midnight had. They were used to being rounded up and didn't seem to mind it. Still, Stevie estimated that she and Stewball brought them in almost twice as fast as John and Peanuts did.

"That horse is about one-half quarter horse and three-quarters sheepdog," Walter remarked as Stevie and Stewball brought in a frisky chestnut mare.

Stevie thought that while Walter's math left something to be desired, he was absolutely right. "He's some horse, isn't he?" she commented proudly, giving Stewball a fond pat. Then Frank pointed out a pinto he wanted brought in, and Stewball darted off in pursuit.

When they had finished, they rode back toward the ranch, herding the auction horses before them. As they reached the edge of the pasture, they saw Kate and Carole waiting at the gate. The two girls waved.

"We thought you'd never get back," Kate called out with a grin.

"Yeah," Carole added. "We've been waiting for ages!"

They swung open the pasture gate, and Kate ran ahead to open the one to the corral. Before long all the horses were inside.

"Guess what job Kate and I just volunteered us all for

next," Carole said, hurrying over to join Stevie and Lisa as they dismounted.

"We're supposed to groom all these horses so they'll look their best for the customers," Kate answered before Stevie and Lisa could guess.

"Great," Stevie said. "But first I want to give Stewball a good grooming. He's been working hard and he deserves it."

She led him into the barn. Lisa followed with Chocolate. Carole and Kate volunteered to take care of the other three horses so that Frank, Walter, and John could get started on the next of the dozen things they had to do before the customers started arriving.

The four girls chatted as they unsaddled and groomed the horses. Stevie and Lisa described their cutting expedition, and Carole and Kate described all the scrumptious things they had helped Phyllis to prepare.

Carole interrupted her praise of Phyllis's secret-recipe blueberry cobbler to comment, "Hey, Stevie, Stewball seems a little restless."

It was true. While the other horses were relaxed and seemed to be enjoying their grooming, Stewball kept impatiently shifting his weight, shaking his head, and generally fussing and fidgeting.

Stevie shrugged. Carole noticed that her friend had a slight frown on her face. But Stevie answered cheerfully enough. "He's still excited about the roundup," she explained. "Besides, Stewball isn't a fussed-over kind of horse."

Lisa raised her eyebrows and glanced at Stewball over Chocolate's back. "That's odd, isn't it? I thought most horses loved to be groomed."

"Remember, Max is always telling us that every horse is an individual," Stevie said. "Stewball just asserts his individuality by not liking to be groomed much. He cares more about how he works than how he looks."

Lisa raised her eyebrows even higher at that, but didn't reply.

"I guess he won't be winning many ribbons in Fitting and Showing back East, will he?" Kate commented quietly. An impeccable grooming was essential to doing well in a Fitting and Showing event in a horse show.

"Don't be silly," Stevie replied with a touch of annoyance in her voice. "He'll stand still to be groomed if he knows it's important. Besides, Stewball will blow them away in the more exciting events. He's already proved how naturally talented he is in dressage and jumping, right?"

"Well, all right," Kate said noncommittally. Stevie didn't seem to notice that it really wasn't much of an answer.

Stevie reached into her pocket and found the sugar lump she had put there at breakfast. Stewball crunched on it happily, standing still long enough for Stevie to complete the grooming hurriedly.

When they had all finished, the girls led the horses out of the barn and across the yard to the pasture gate.

"Good job this morning, Stewball," Stevie told the horse, giving him a quick hug before releasing him into the pasture. "Now your reward is that you get to play with your friends for the rest of the day."

As if understanding her words, Stewball raised his head and sniffed the air, apparently trying to locate the herd. Stevie's eyes were glued to the horse. She was spellbound by how free he looked as he gazed out over his domain, his mane softly ruffled by the slight morning breeze. Finally Stewball found the smell he was looking for. He snorted, shook his head, and broke into a frolicking gallop toward the herd, which was just visible on a rise of land across the pasture. The other four horses followed Stewball's lead as he let out a whinny.

"He's such a happy horse, isn't he," Stevie remarked. Since it wasn't really a question, the others didn't answer, though each of them had to agree that it was true.

Carole found herself wondering once again whether Stewball could ever be truly happy spending most of his life in a barn in Virginia. She also wondered whether Stevie was wondering the same thing. The expression on Stevie's face at the moment was inscrutable.

Then all thoughts of Stewball were erased, from Carole's mind at least, as the girls returned to the corral. "Where do we start?" she wondered, looking at the group of horses.

"Let's just wade right in," Kate said. She and Carole had already brought out the grooming tools and left them just outside the corral gate. The four girls picked them up and headed into the corral.

Soon they had chosen their first customers and brought

them over to the unofficial "beauty salon"—actually just a spot along the corral fence. Carole's first horse was a compact bay gelding. Lisa's was a frisky chestnut. Stevie had singled out Midnight, the mischievous black gelding. Kate had picked a tall gray roan.

"Nobody is going to be buying these horses for their grooming," Kate told the others. "But it's always a good idea to show a horse off to his best advantage for a sale."

"Besides, this will be a good opportunity for us to get some idea of the horses' personalities," Carole pointed out. She ran a hand down the bay's front leg, lifted his foot, and began cleaning his hoof out. "For instance, this fellow has just shown me that he's well trained and calm. He lifted his foot without any problem."

"That's right," Kate said. "Different horses have different things that upset them, different things that make them happy, and different skills and ability. Like Stevie was saying earlier, horses are as individual as people. We want to be able to give buyers a sense of what they're getting."

"I already know that Midnight here should go to a rider with a sense of humor," Stevie commented, "because he's definitely got one himself."

"And I know that Lucky is very precise and obedient," Kate said, patting the gray roan she was grooming. "Actually, I knew that already, because I helped a lot with his training. He's young, but he's great at taking direction from a rider—he'll follow any signal he's given, no matter how complicated, no questions asked."

"Really?" Carole said, glancing with new appreciation at the horse. "He's so elegant looking, too. He doesn't really look like a typical Western horse."

"I agree," Kate said, beginning to go over Lucky's coat with a stiff brush. "He'd probably do great in the show ring back East. In fact, I already have a buyer in mind for him."

"How'd he get his name?" Lisa asked.

"Look at his face," Kate said, turning the horse a little so the others could see. Lucky had a white stripe running down his nose. The stripe was narrow and fairly straight except at the top, where it angled off sharply to the left across his forehead. "We thought his stripe looked like a number seven. So we started calling him that—Lucky Seven, that is. Lucky for short."

"It's perfect," Carole said, and the others agreed.

As the girls finished the first set of horses and moved on to others, they continued to compare notes about them. Lisa and Stevie found a bay mare who was very gentle and docile —Lisa recognized her as Ellie, the first horse she and Chocolate had cut from the herd the other day. They decided that Ellie would be ideal for a family with young children.

Carole worked on a beautiful golden palomino mare the wranglers called Goldie, who was young, spirited, and high-strung. Carole thought that Goldie should go to an experienced rider who was willing to take a little more time with her training.

Stevie groomed a short pinto pony. Kate told her he was called Road Map because of his distinctive markings. Stevie could tell that Road Map was lively and strong but well trained and very smart. She thought that those qualities, along with his small size, would make him the perfect choice for a young person who was a better-than-average rider.

There was a fast, obedient Appaloosa gelding named Amigo who Kate was sure would be just right for a working cowboy or a rodeo rider. A bay named Rocky seemed best suited to be a cutting horse because of his quickness. And Kate and Carole between them had some trouble restraining a very spirited yet skittish mare called the Red Queen. She was a very tall and slim chestnut with a fine head and arched neck, which made Carole think she had at least a little Arabian in her bloodlines. The girls decided the mare should definitely go to a very experienced rider.

Finally the last of the horses was groomed to perfection. The girls leaned on the corral fence to rest and admire their work. Carole thought the horses looked wonderful, and that the buyers would be clamoring for them. She told the others so, and they agreed without hesitation. They were proud of the grooming they'd done, which as Kate had pointed out would show the horses to their best advantage. But they also had to admit that the horses themselves were beautiful and wonderful and well trained. They decided it was a great combination.

After a few minutes they left the corral and headed off in search of more ways to be helpful. It was almost noon, and the customers would start arriving right after lunch. There was no time to waste.

THE BUYERS BEGAN arriving right on schedule. The Devines and their guests had finished everything that needed to be done just in time, eaten a hurried but well-deserved lunch, and headed back outside as the first car pulled into the drive. The girls helped Phyllis carry out the lemonade, cookies, pies, and other goodies, and they promised to take turns helping her sell them. Luckily the food booth had a good view of the auction platform, because The Saddle Club didn't want to miss a second of the auction when it started. Lisa and Kate took the first shift, and Stevie and Carole headed over to the corral.

Before Frank began auctioning off the horses, the buyers had a chance to look them over. John, Walter, Stevie, and Carole stood by to bring out individual horses when requested so potential buyers could examine them more carefully. Stevie's first customer was a man with two little girls about five and six years old.

"Hi, there," she greeted them.

"Hi! We're getting a horse!" the younger girl announced.

The man patted her on the head. "I think she could probably guess that, Nina," he said with a laugh. Then he turned to Stevie. "My daughters have been promised their very own horse. They're pretty new riders. Can you recommend one of these beasts for them?"

"As a matter of fact, I know the perfect horse," Stevie answered without hesitation. "Wait right here, I'll bring her out." She entered the corral and returned a moment later leading Ellie, the gentle bay mare.

"Oh, she's pretty!" exclaimed the older girl. "Is she a girl? We want a girl."

"Yes, she's a mare," Stevie told her. "That's a girl horse. Her name is Ellie."

The man quickly checked the mare over. Ellie stood docilely while he lifted all four feet, looked in her mouth, and ran his hands over her. Stevie suspected he knew what he was doing. "Do you have any other horses?" she asked him.

"You bet," he replied. "My stepson is a rodeo rider. He's seventeen. And my wife and I ride as well. But none of our horses is right for Lucy and Nina here—they've been learning to ride on an ancient nag that lives on a farm a couple of miles down the road. Now they think they're ready for a horse of their own."

"We are, Daddy!" the older girl, Lucy, insisted. Ellie had

116

lowered her head to sniff at the girls, and Lucy was patting the mare's velvety soft nose while Nina smoothed back her mane. Stevie could tell that both girls were already in love.

"You know, I just got my very own horse, too," Stevie told Lucy and Nina. "His name is Stewball."

"That's nice. We want to get this one," Nina said, patting Ellie. "She's pretty."

"That's true," Stevie agreed. "But there's more to picking a good horse than just finding one that's pretty, you know. I think Ellie may be just the right horse for you two—not just because she's pretty, but also because she's gentle and patient, and because she'll be able to teach you to be even better riders than you already are."

"Really?" Lucy said, gazing at Ellie with new respect. "I want to be a really good rider, just like my big brother."

"Me, too!" Nina chimed in. "I want to be a rodeo rider just like him."

Stevie smiled. The sisters reminded her of herself when she was their age. She had been just as enthusiastic and eager to learn. "I'm sure you'll both be great riders before long," she told them. "Ellie will be able to help you develop all the skills you need, like communicating through the reins and with your legs, keeping your balance in the saddle, things like that."

"She sure is pretty," Lucy said reverently, still staring at Ellie.

Stevie nodded and chuckled. The little girls were too caught up in the excitement of getting their own horse to worry about practical things like balance. She could understand that—very well, in fact. Didn't she feel exactly the same way about Stewball?

That thought startled her a little. She found herself wondering just how different her decision to buy Stewball was from the little girls' decision about Ellie. They had decided they wanted Ellie because she was pretty. Were Stevie's reasons for wanting Stewball any more logical?

The girls' father had finished his examination. "Well, she seems to be in good shape. And it looks as though she's gentle."

"Oh, she is," Stevie assured him, trying to forget her thoughts about Stewball. "She's a real sweetheart. And very obedient, too."

The man nodded, looking satisfied, and Stevie had the feeling she'd just made a sale. She was glad, too, because she was convinced that Ellie and the little girls would be a perfect match.

The girls and their father said good-bye and wandered off toward the refreshment table, and Stevie turned to help a man who had been waiting patiently.

For the next hour or so they were all kept busy answering questions, showing horses, and selling Phyllis's delicious baked goods and lemonade. When they were sure that all the customers had had a chance to check over the horses, the auction began. Frank acted as official auctioneer. He stood on a large, sturdy wooden platform that John and Walter had built. A wide, gently sloping ramp led up to it from one side, and as each horse came up for sale, John or Walter would lead it up onto the platform so the buyers had a good view. The buyers were seated in rows of folding chairs that John had set up in the yard between the corral and the house.

By this time Stevie and Carole were taking their turn at the refreshment table. Lisa and Kate took up a position behind the platform so they could tell Frank what they knew about each horse's personality as it was led up the ramp.

The first horse auctioned off was Amigo, the Appaloosa. John led the gelding carefully up the ramp. Amigo followed without hesitation and stood quietly, gazing out over the crowd gathered below as if he were shopping for the perfect owner.

"Hello there, folks, and welcome to The Bar None Ranch," Frank began. He wasn't using a microphone, but his deep voice carried easily to everyone, including Phyllis, Stevie, and Carole, who were watching from the refreshment table. "I'm Frank Devine. On behalf of myself, my family, and everyone here at The Bar None, we're glad you could all make it. As you've already seen, we have some fine animals for sale today. And as you can probably tell already, I don't sound much like a professional auctioneer, but I'll do my best."

The Saddle Club girls giggled. With his relaxed drawl Frank sounded nothing like a fast-talking auctioneer. If Carole hadn't known better, she would have thought he was a lifelong rancher instead of a retired Marine.

"I'm lucky to have some good help," Frank added. He gestured at Kate and Lisa. "These girls know the horses inside out and upside down, and they'll be helping me to tell you a little bit about each animal's character and abilities so you'll have a better chance of making a good choice. And if any horse isn't exactly what they and I say it is, I'll be happy to take it back for a full refund."

"I guess we'd better know what we're talking about, then," Lisa whispered.

"Don't worry," Kate replied. "We do."

"We'll start with this horse in front of me," Frank continued. Amigo had been standing quietly through Frank's introduction. Now John led him in a tight circle on the platform as Frank described him. "He's a gelding, part quarter horse, and about eight years old, near as we can tell."

He leaned over to listen to Kate for a moment, then continued. "My daughter Kate tells me he's called Amigo, and that he'll be a real friend to any hardworking cowboy or experienced rodeo rider out there. He's smart and steady and strong, and he's trained within an inch of his life. He'll be a star performer on the range or in the rodeo ring."

Frank paused for a moment to let all this information sink in. "Now, what do I hear for him?"

Bids came fast and furious for several minutes. Amigo obviously had several would-be owners in the crowd. Finally the bidding was narrowed down to two people. The Saddle

Club was happy to see that both bidders looked like experienced cowboys. After several more bids one of the men dropped out with a tip of his hat to the other.

"Sold, to the gentleman in the blue shirt," Frank said finally. "I don't have a gavel, but that's official, folks."

John led Amigo back down the ramp. The Appaloosa's new owner made his way through the crowd to meet them. From her position behind the platform, Lisa watched them for a moment, pleased with the way the sale had turned out.

But soon her attention returned to the action in front of her. Walter had just led Ellie onto the platform.

"Hi, there, you two," came a voice from behind her. Lisa and Kate turned to see Stevie grinning at them. Carole and Christine were with her.

"Is it our turn at the food booth already?" Lisa asked, a little disappointed.

"No way," Carole assured her. "Christine's parents brought her over. As soon as they got here, they insisted on filling in for us so we could come over and join you."

Meanwhile Frank had started his spiel. "Ellie here is a mare, about ten years old," he said. "She's well trained and obedient."

Stevie reached over and tugged at the cuff of Frank's jeans. When he leaned over, she whispered in his ear. He nodded and stood up again.

"One of my expert helpers has just told me that Ellie is very gentle and patient," he said. "She's a good, steady horse, and as you can see, she's on the small side. For all those reasons she would be ideal as a first horse for kids."

In the audience Stevie spotted Lucy and Nina. They were both jumping up and down eagerly, hanging on to their father's hands. "That's the one, Daddy!" Lucy cried loudly. "That's Ellie, she's ours!"

A ripple of laughter ran through the audience. Everyone had heard the little girl. When her father finally pulled his hand free to bid, nobody bid against him. Stevie smiled. She wasn't surprised that nobody dared to bid on the mare after hearing Lucy's comment!

"Sold," Frank announced after waiting a moment. He smiled down at Lucy and Nina. "To the two young ladies in the front row."

"I'm glad Ellie came out early," Stevie told her friends. "Now those girls can relax and enjoy the rest of the auction knowing that they've already got their dream horse!"

The others nodded. But there was no time to discuss it further; John was already leading the next horse onto the ramp.

One horse after another was auctioned off. The girls thought that the amount of money people were bidding was just about perfect. The prices were high enough that the Devines would make a terrific profit from the auction, but low enough that people could feel they'd gotten a bargain on a well-trained animal.

Another thing that seemed even more perfect to The Saddle Club was that the horses seemed to be getting matched up with appropriate owners. They watched as a woman whom Kate recognized as an outstanding local horsewoman bought Goldie, the spirited palomino. And they nodded in satisfaction when the same woman bought Road Map for her young daughter.

"Even though she's only eight, and small for her age, she's practically an expert rider already," Kate told the others. "You should see her ride. Road Map will be perfect for her."

A little later Rocky went to a wrangler who worked at a nearby ranch. Then it was Midnight's turn.

"Now, my helpers tell me this horse is very special," Frank told the audience. "He needs someone who will appreciate his, uh, special sense of humor. And he needs a good rider who can handle him—he's pretty frisky."

Several people bid on him, but Midnight ended up going to a teenage boy. Stevie had noticed the boy examining Midnight earlier. "Do you know him?" she asked Kate.

"I recognize him," she replied. "He goes to my school. His name is Mac. He's a senior, and he's pretty_ well-known around school for two reasons. The first is that he's quite a good calf roper. He's taken some prizes in local rodeos."

"What's the other reason?" Carole asked.

Kate grinned. "He's even more famous—or should I say infamous—for being the class clown."

"Perfect!" Stevie exclaimed happily. She looked at Midnight's new owner with greater respect.

As the day went on, things continued in pretty much the same fashion. Every horse seemed custom-made for the rider who bought it—although the girls preferred to think of things the other way around! Finally the last horse, Lucky, was led onto the platform. Frank described the gelding's qualities, including Kate's recommendation that he be considered for English show riding. Half a dozen people bid on him, but in the end a tall, middle-aged man dressed in a suit and tie bought him.

"He doesn't look much like a show rider," Stevie said, a little disappointed. Lucky was a terrific horse, and he deserved a rider who would appreciate him.

"He's not," Kate said. "But he is the person I was thinking of when I said I knew who should buy Lucky."

"What do you mean?" Lisa asked.

"He's an agent for a stable back East," Kate explained. "I was talking to one of my old trainers. He happened to be looking around for a couple of new horses, and when I told him about Lucky, he decided to send that man out here to look at him and maybe buy him." She nodded at the man, who was stroking Lucky while talking to Walter. "He may not look much like a rider, but he knows what he's doing."

"What a relief," Carole said. "I thought our perfect record was going to be broken."

"We have managed to match up horses and riders pretty well, haven't we?" said Lisa.

Kate nodded. "But the important thing about that isn't our record. It's the fact that the horses *and* their new owners will be happy and able to get the best out of each other."

"That's true," Stevie agreed. She thought about Lucy and

Nina and what a perfect teacher Ellie would be for them—and what loving owners they would be to her. She thought about Midnight, whose abilities *and* sense of humor seemed perfectly matched to his owner's. She thought about Lucky, who would be going East where his talents could be put to their best use. And then she thought about herself and Stewball. Were they as good a match?

Stevie remained deep in thought as she and her friends went to help Frank and Phyllis wrap things up.

As THE GIRLS were helping John fold and stack the chairs, a horse van pulled into the driveway. Frank hurried over. "Stevie, there's the van that's going to be taking the horses out East. You'd better go out and round up Stewball; we're going to start loading right now."

Stevie bit her lip. There was a long pause. "That's okay, Frank," she said quietly at last. "I changed my mind. I'm leaving him here."

Stevie's voice was so low that the others weren't sure they'd heard her correctly. "What do you mean, leaving him here?" Carole demanded.

"If I don't ship him now, it could be a while before I can arrange to get him out to you," Frank said.

"I've decided not to buy him at all," Stevie said. "I'm sorry I waited until the last minute to tell you, and I hope that doesn't cause any problems for you, but I'm not taking him."

"That's no problem for me," Frank said. "Stewball is a

125

good worker and we'd be happy to keep him. But what made you change your mind?"

Stevie thought for a second. She had just figured the whole thing out herself, and she wanted to be sure to explain it so the others would understand, too. "Stewball belongs here at The Bar None," she explained. "He should spend the rest of his life doing what he does best, cutting and herding. And he should be rewarded for his hard work by being able to do what he loves best, playing with the rest of his herd out on the range."

"Well, I can't say I'm not surprised," Frank said, rubbing his chin. "I really thought you had your heart set on having him. But I can certainly understand your reasoning. So Stewball stays." He nodded and then left to help Walter load the Eastern-bound horses onto the van.

Carole, Lisa, Christine, and Kate were speechless for a moment, still trying to take in what had just happened. John did not have the same problem, however.

"Congratulations, Stevie," he said. "I'm glad you finally came to your senses."

Stevie frowned and seemed about to take offense at the comment. But then she shrugged and relaxed. "I guess you were right all along," she said. "It took me a while to realize that even though Stewball is perfect for me to ride when I'm here, he might not be perfect for me to take back to Virginia."

"I think you made the right decision, Stevie," Kate told her. The other girls nodded.

"Thanks, you guys," Stevie said, looking a little sad. She folded the last two chairs and added them to the stack against the barn wall. A truck would be coming to pick them up soon. "I guess we're finished here. The auction is really over."

"That's right," John said. He brushed off his hands. "I'll be in the barn if anybody needs me." He walked away toward the barn door. Lisa thought he might have realized that Stevie needed to be alone with her friends for a minute, and she thought again how sensitive he could be sometimes.

Carole put an arm around Stevie's shoulder. "Are you sure you're okay with this? I know how much you were looking forward to owning Stewball."

"I think so," Stevie said. "It was hard, but I'm pretty sure I made the right decision. All day I've been watching people choose horses who are suited to their personalities *and* their needs, and I've been thinking about that. Those two little girls started me thinking about it when they decided they wanted Ellie. That gelding, Midnight, made me think about it more when I worried that he might not go to an owner who would really appreciate everything about him. And then when I saw that Lucky—who really will make a wonderful show horse—was going East where he belonged, I knew what I had to do. Lucky belongs there, but Stewball belongs here. He *needs* to be here to be happy."

The others were silent for a moment. There was nothing more to say on the subject right then, and they all knew it. Finally Lisa spoke. "I can hardly believe our visit is just about over." They were scheduled to leave early the next morning.

"I know," Stevie agreed. "So much has happened on this trip."

"Isn't that how it always is when you three come out here?" Kate teased. "Even if nothing is happening at all, you manage to stir things up."

They all laughed. "I guess that's true," Carole admitted. "But you can't say we're not fun!"

"True," Kate said. "So what fun thing do we want to do now? We've got an hour or so before dinner."

"I'd better say my good-byes now," Christine said. "I imagine my parents are about ready to go." She hugged the three Eastern girls, promising to write. Then she hurried off to find her parents.

"I'm going to go out and find the herd," Stevie told the others. "I want to say good-bye to Stewball. I may not have time in the morning."

Her friends watched her go. Then Carole turned to Kate. "You know who I'd like to say good-bye to?"

"Moon Glow and Felix?" Kate guessed.

"Bingo!" Carole replied with a smile. She turned to Lisa. "Want to come along?"

"Uh, I might be over in a few minutes," Lisa said. "I have something else to do first." She'd been hoping to find a chance to say good-bye to John in private. It was strange to think that the next day they would be thousands of miles apart.

John looked up as Lisa entered the saddle storage area. "Hi, there," he greeted her, his smile warm and welcoming. He hung up the bridle he was holding. Then he grabbed Lisa by the hand and gently pulled her over to a large trunk. They sat down on it side by side, so close their knees were touching. "I was afraid I wouldn't see you again before you left."

"Well, here I am," Lisa replied with a smile. "I didn't want to go without saying good-bye."

"I'm glad." John smiled down at her. He was still holding her hand.

Lisa took a deep breath. "Listen, John, we should keep in touch after I go home," she began hurriedly. "It will be hard to stay friends from such a distance, but we can write to each other. And I'm sure I'll visit The Bar None again before long—"

"Lisa," John interrupted her gently. "I don't know if we should try so hard. I mean, I've really liked spending time with you, and I hope you do come back here again real soon. I've never met anybody like you, and I've never met anybody I've liked as much."

"Same here," Lisa said quietly, looking down at her hand clasped in his.

"What we've got is a really nice, really special friendship," John continued. "We shouldn't mess it up with a lot of promises that might be hard to keep."

Lisa bit her lip and nodded. Even though what John was

saying made her sad, it also made a lot of sense. "I guess you're right," she admitted. "I guess it would be hard to, well, you know . . ."

"I know," John said. He leaned forward, and Lisa closed her eyes for one last kiss.

15

"IT'S LIKE WE never left," Stevie groaned, leaning on her pitchfork.

"Well, not quite," Carole said with a smile.

Stevie, Carole, and Lisa were back at Pine Hollow once again. And once again they were mucking out stalls in the summer heat. The difference was that this time they were in a much better mood.

Stevie got back to work. "You're right. Even if we're stuck cleaning out these stalls, at least now we can think back on the great time we had at The Bar None."

"True," Lisa agreed dreamily. "And we can look forward to the next time we go back." She let out a sigh. Stevie and Carole looked at her curiously.

"Are we missing something here, Lisa?" Stevie asked. "Why do you look so funny?"

Carole gasped and put a hand to her mouth. "It's John, right?" she exclaimed. "I meant to keep an eye out to see if things were going well between you two. But with all the excitement about the auction, and Stevie buying Stewball and everything—I guess I forgot all about it."

Lisa blushed. "Don't worry. Things went well."

"Really?" Stevie said. "Does this mean he's your boyfriend now? That's so romantic!"

"No, he's not my boyfriend," Lisa said. "We're just good friends. It would be too hard to be boyfriend and girlfriend over such a long distance."

Stevie shrugged. "I guess you're right, although it *would* be pretty romantic. . . ."

"And difficult," Lisa finished for her. She sighed again and smiled. "No, he's not my boyfriend. But we had an awfully nice time while I was there."

After a little more urging, her friends managed to drag the whole story out of her—kisses and all.

"Bob Harris will be jealous if he finds out," Carole commented. "I still can't believe this was all going on right under my nose—*again*," she added, shaking her head in wonder.

"I can believe that," Stevie said. "I just can't believe *I* didn't notice."

Carole gave her a withering look. "I can *definitely* believe that. You only had eyes for Stewball." She grinned. "By the way, Stevie, I'm glad to see that you're not holding any

132

grudges about what we did. We were sure you'd be annoyed when you realized."

"Realized what?" Stevie asked, looking mystified.

Carole and Lisa looked at each other. "You know," Lisa said. "The way we worked so hard to show you that Stewball wasn't the right horse for you to have at Pine Hollow."

Stevie stopped working and gazed at her friends in surprise. "You did?"

"You mean you didn't even notice?" Carole exclaimed. She and Lisa burst out laughing.

"So much for that Saddle Club project!" Lisa said. She and Carole took turns explaining their scheme to convince Stevie that Stewball was a Western horse at heart.

"Well, that was an okay plan," Stevie commented when they had finished. "But it would have been better if I'd been in on it."

Carole and Lisa laughed. They were relieved that Stevie wasn't annoyed. "By the way, Stevie, if you're finished with that stall, Max wants us to do Romeo's before Polly brings him in from their trail ride," Lisa said.

"Okay, I'll do it," Stevie said agreeably. She finished spreading out the straw in the stall she had just finished cleaning and then headed across the corridor to Romeo's.

Carole waited for her to start grumbling. "Aren't you still mad that Polly has her own horse and you don't?" Carole asked when she realized that no grumbling was forthcoming from Stevie, at least not at the moment.

"No," Stevie said absentmindedly. "You know, I think I

figured out something important on that trip. I realized that it's really important to look for a partnership that's good in every possible way."

"You mean you and Stewball weren't a good partnership because your interest is in English riding and his talents are for Western?" Carole guessed.

"Exactly," Stevie said. "And more than that—he never could have been as happy an English horse as he is a Western one. That fact was like the one piece of a puzzle that doesn't fit." She shrugged. "I guess I just kind of took that stuff for granted. It's probably because you and Starlight are so perfect for each other, and Phil and Teddy too."

"Sometimes there's just one thing that keeps something from being perfect," Lisa said thoughtfully. Stevie and Carole had the feeling she wasn't talking about Stewball. When she started blushing again, they knew they were right. Lisa was thinking about John, and how they could possibly have been more than just good friends if they didn't live so far apart.

Stevie decided not to ask her and embarrass her further. Instead she kept the conversation on Stewball. "The bottom line is, I had to do what I did because I knew it would be best for him. I had to put his needs ahead of my wish to own him."

"And you don't regret it?" Carole asked. She stepped out of the stall she had just finished and leaned on the open half door of Romeo's to talk to Stevie.

"No way," Stevie said. "I'm very happy with my decision.

And after all, I can still ride Stewball whenever we go to The Bar None." She began to whistle as she worked.

Carole was a little surprised that Stevie was taking this so well. "But you still don't have your own horse," she said. "I can't believe you're not just a little bit upset about that."

"Yeah," Lisa agreed, joining Carole outside Romeo's stall. "You came so close to getting one. It must be awfully disappointing."

Stevie stopped whistling and grinned. "Nope," she replied. Then she started whistling again.

Carole and Lisa exchanged a glance. "How can you say that?" Carole asked. "I thought you really wanted your own horse."

"I do," Stevie said. "But think about it. If I convinced my parents to buy me a horse this time, it shouldn't be too hard to break them down when the *really* perfect right horse comes along. It's just a matter of time."

"True," Carole agreed. She hadn't thought of it that way. "So I guess all you really have to do is find the perfect horse and you're all set."

Lisa smiled. "Now *that's* a Saddle Club project worth working on!"

ABOUT THE AUTHOR

BONNIE BRYANT is the author of more than a hundred books about horses, including The Saddle Club series, Saddle Club Super Editions, the Pony Tails series, and Pine Hollow, which follows the Saddle Club girls into their teens. She has also written novels and movie novelizations under her married name, B. B. Hiller.

Ms. Bryant began writing The Saddle Club in 1986. Although she had done some riding before that, she intensified her studies then and found herself learning right along with her characters Stevie, Carole, and Lisa. She claims that they are all much better riders than she is.

Ms. Bryant was born and raised in New York City. She still lives there, in Greenwich Village, with her two sons.

Help your friend get FREE books and FREE gifts - by joining The Saddle Club!

As an official Saddle Club member, you'll get:

- A beautiful keepsake diary
- An official Saddle Club poster
- A stunning charm bracelet and Saddle Club charms
- Plus much, much more!